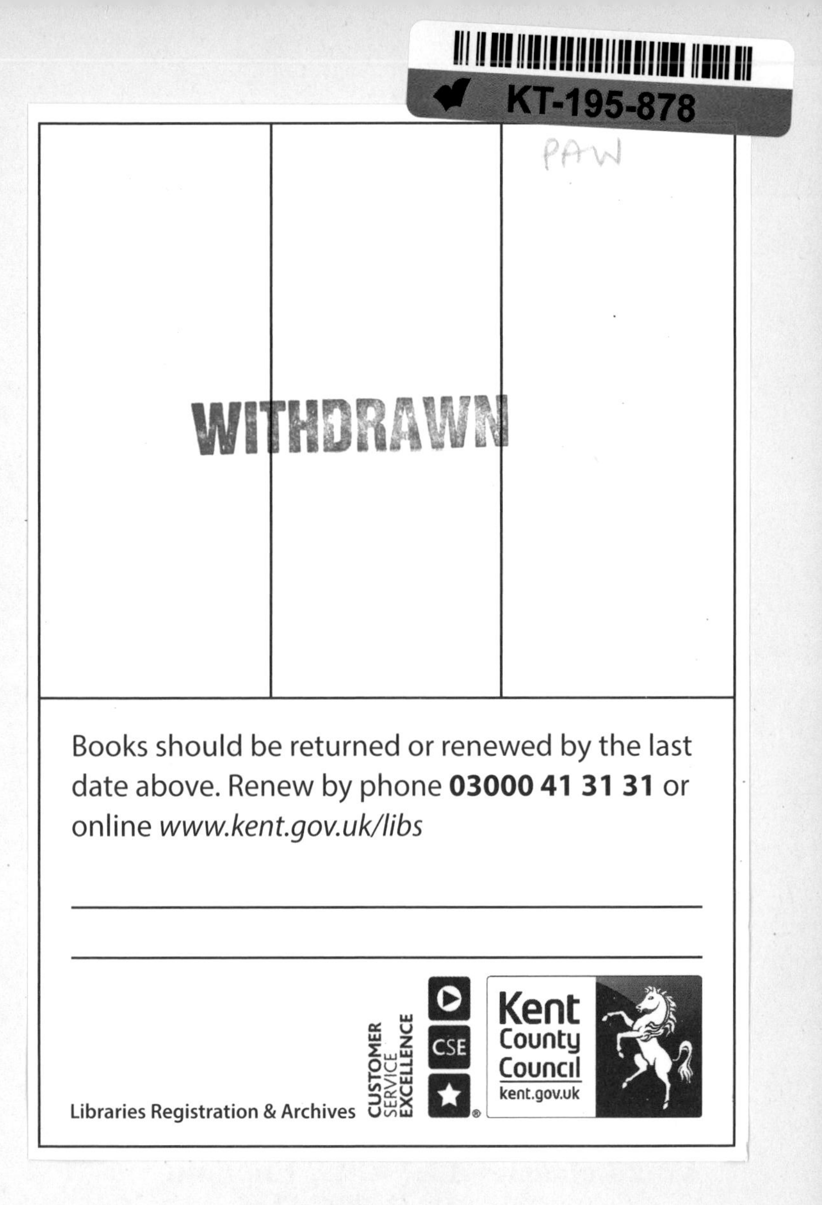

KT-195-878
PAW
WITHDRAWN
Books should be returned or renewed by the last date above. Renew by phone 03000 41 31 31 or online www.kent.gov.uk/libs
Libraries Registration & Archives
CUSTOMER SERVICE EXCELLENCE
CSE
Kent County Council
kent.gov.uk

C161019844

SPECIAL MESSAGE TO READERS

THE ULVERSCROFT FOUNDATION
(registered UK charity number 264873)

was established in 1972 to provide funds for research, diagnosis and treatment of eye diseases. Examples of major projects funded by the Ulverscroft Foundation are:-

- The Children's Eye Unit at Moorfields Eye Hospital, London
- The Ulverscroft Children's Eye Unit at Great Ormond Street Hospital for Sick Children
- Funding research into eye diseases and treatment at the Department of Ophthalmology, University of Leicester
- The Ulverscroft Vision Research Group, Institute of Child Health
- Twin operating theatres at the Western Ophthalmic Hospital, London
- The Chair of Ophthalmology at the Royal Australian College of Ophthalmologists

You can help further the work of the Foundation by making a donation or leaving a legacy. Every contribution is gratefully received. If you would like to help support the Foundation or require further information, please contact:

PATTERN FOR SURVIVAL

Dr. Villiers is one of the country's leading missile research scientists. When he disappears, the alarmed British Intelligence are quick to send in their top agent to investigate. Steve Carradine is able to recover the scientist before Russian agents can smuggle him out of the country, but the affair turns out to be part of an even larger conspiracy . . . And unless Carradine can penetrate to the heart of the mystery and take out the mastermind behind it, the safety of the entire western world is in jeopardy!

Books by Manning K. Robertson
in the Linford Mystery Library:

SEEK AND DESTROY
THE SECRET ENEMY
BLUEPRINT FOR DESTRUCTION
TWELVE HOURS TO DESTINY

MANNING K. ROBERTSON

PATTERN FOR SURVIVAL

Complete and Unabridged

LINFORD
Leicester

First published in Great Britain

First Linford Edition
published 2015

A catalogue record for this book is available from the British Library.

ISBN 978–1–4448–2484–1

Published by
F. A. Thorpe (Publishing)
Anstey, Leicestershire

Set by Words & Graphics Ltd.
Anstey, Leicestershire
Printed and bound in Great Britain by
T. J. International Ltd., Padstow, Cornwall

This book is printed on acid-free paper

1

Trouble and Treason

Punctually, at nine o'clock, the black limousine drove up to the high barbed-wire-topped gates and stopped smoothly. The powerful engine purred softly beneath the bonnet. A second later the door of the security block opened and an official stepped out and came forward. He paused, bending forward at the window of the car, and gave a brisk nod as he recognised the occupant.

'Good evening, Dr. Grayson.' A faint trace of surprise tinged the other's voice. 'We didn't expect you back for another two days.'

'I didn't expect to be back so early, Forbes.' John Grayson, D.Sc., F.Inst.P., shrugged his shoulders, hands resting on the wheel. 'But it seems they cannot get along without me. Do you know if Dr. Villiers is still on the site?'

'I'll check that for you, sir.' Forbes moved back into the security building. The gate swung back and Grayson eased the car forward until he had drawn level with the half-open window. Inside the building he could see Forbes checking through the rows of security badges, each carrying the photograph of its owner. He came out a few moments later and handed Grayson's badge to him. 'You'll find Dr. Villiers in his office, sir. I've buzzed him. He's waiting for you.'

'Thanks.' Grayson pressed his foot gently on the accelerator and drove into the grounds of the missile research station. On one side of the narrow road was a stretch of barbed wire looking out onto open moorland. On the other were the twin rows of office blocks and research laboratories; and further back, almost hidden in the purple dusk, he could make out the huge concrete buildings, more than a hundred feet high, in which the climatic storage trials of the huge rockets were carried out. A few lights showed in the windows of the research block and there were one or two in the main office block. Turning the car off the main road running like a major artery through the site, he stopped in front of the offices, switched off the ignition and got out, slamming the door behind him.

Going through the entrance of the block, he closed the door softly behind him. The corridor was cool in front of him, or perhaps it was the very pale blue of the walls which gave the impression of coolness. Grayson made his way swiftly along the corridor, stepped into the lift at the far end and punched the button for the fourth floor. Even the smooth ride up in the lift seemed to be charged with a special significance this evening. Grayson was aware of it as he watched the palely illuminated floors slip past outside the metal grill, just as he was aware of the presence of the small glass phial which now reposed in his waistcoat pocket, within easy reach of his fingers. He knew exactly how to use it. Varandashky had given him explicit instructions, making absolutely certain he understood them, before parting with the phial. He smiled grimly to himself and the faint light outside the lift slid smoothly to a stop at the fourth floor. One had to admit that the Reds had an organisation which functioned far better and more efficiently than anything he had ever known in Britain.

There was a riot of thoughts and ideas racing through his mind as he paused for a long moment at the entrance to the lift. Then, with an effort, he deliberately closed his mind to the chaos and concentrated on what he had to say; what he had to do once he met Villiers. There was nothing else in his mind as he walked along the short passage and stopped in front of the door at the far end. The glass panel glowed faintly with the reflected light from behind. There was also a narrow bar of light showing under the door.

Grayson rapped sharply on the door, waited for a moment and then went inside. The office was empty, but the light still burned on the desk and there were papers scattered over it indicating that Villiers was still around somewhere;

otherwise they would all have been securely locked away in the heavy-duty steel filing cabinets against the wall.

A moment later, the door leading to the inner office opened and Villiers came in. He glanced up sharply, then relaxed visibly as he saw who it was. 'You startled me, John. Security said you were on your way up. How did the holiday go?'

Grayson smiled faintly, lowered himself into the vacant chair in front of the desk and stretched his legs out lazily in front of him. Every action was as smooth and relaxed as Villiers would expect it to be. Above all, the other must suspect nothing until it was too late for him to be able to do anything about it.

'It made a break from the usual routine, I suppose. Little more than that.'

Villiers nodded, placed the neat sheaf of papers on the walnut desk in front of him and sat down, placing his elbows on the papers and leaning forward and resting his weight on them. He closed his eyes and pinched together the flesh at the bridge of his nose. 'The trouble with this kind of work is that it inevitably restricts where you can go on holiday.' He pushed the papers to one side as if he had just remembered they were there. 'Funny, you know. Before I came into this job, we used to go to Yugoslavia nearly every year. Once we went as far as Yalta. You'd like it there. Mediterranean-type climate but without the crowds you get in the south of France. No more of that, I'm afraid, at least until I resign or retire and the government security boys are sure I can't give away any vital information to the Reds.'

He leaned back and clasped his hands behind his head, staring up at the ceiling for a moment. Then he glanced down again, looking sharply at Grayson. His brows were knit in a straight line of concentration. 'You're not supposed to report back for another two days, are you? What happened? Something come up, or — ?'

'Nothing happened,' said Grayson easily. For a moment he felt sure he had seen a flare of suspicion in the other's eyes. It did not really surprise him. In an establishment such as this, with the government tightening security every month, it was only to be expected that anything out of the ordinary, no matter how innocent it might seem on the surface, would be examined by each of his colleagues, just to make sure there was no ulterior motive behind his actions. What was Forbes doing at that moment? he wondered vaguely. Sitting in the security block drinking the inevitable cup of coffee, or checking further on him? He pushed the idea out of his mind. There was no reason whatsoever to believe that anyone suspected him of anything.

'It turned out to be boring even after the end of the first week. Then the weather broke and we decided to come back. I thought I'd pop in this evening — ' He smiled faintly. ' — just to break myself in again.'

Villiers shrugged. He seemed to accept the other's explanation. As Grayson's immediate superior, and the man in charge of the special research station, his manner was business-like and calculating. 'I can't say I'm really sorry that you're back.' He took his hands from behind his neck and placed them flat on the desk, shoulders hunched a little. The eyes behind the horn-rimmed glasses had taken on a fixed look. 'We have been having trouble lately. You saw the beginning of it just before you went on leave.' His lips curled a little. 'In fact, if we knew how much trouble we were going to have, you might not have had your leave.'

Grayson raised his brows a little. Deep inside, he had the impatient feeling that the seconds and minutes were ticking away more rapidly than he liked. There was a lot to be done, but above all he must not arouse the other's suspicions. As Varandashky had impressed on him, there must be no slip-up in what he had to do. To hurry things along could lead to a mistake. Since security had been tightened up around the establishment, anything even remotely suspicious would be spotted at once. He may already have started a chain of suspicion all down the line by arriving there at this time of the evening and two days earlier than he was supposed to report back for duty. Only the fact that he was one of the topmost scientists at the station might have stood him in good stead and allayed any suspicions. That, and the fact that so far only two people knew he was on the site.

'Just what's the trouble, sir?'

'The recent test firings have been far below specification. Thrust, specific impulse — the lot. We shall have to get it together, in detail, as soon as you get back.'

'If it's as important as that, why don't we make a start now?' Grayson suggested.

'Well, I . . . Certainly, if you're sure you can spare the time.'

Grayson smiled thinly. 'This job is beginning to get into my blood, just as it is in yours.'

'I'll take that as a compliment, John,' he said. 'All right then, I'll get out all of the relevant papers and we can go through them. It looks as if we shall have to start from square one again though. I've had Merrills go through them twice. There doesn't seem to be anything superficial that we've missed. It's looking more and more as if the trouble is fundamental.'

There was a moment's silence, then

Villiers scraped back his chair and went over to the filing cabinets, pulling a bunch of keys from his trouser pocket.

Grayson watched him narrowly. As the other unlocked the drawer and took out the file with the large red words TOP SECRET stamped across the top right-hand corner, he got up and took off his overcoat, hung it on the peg and unbuttoned his jacket. 'May as well make myself comfortable,' he said. 'If this is as bad as you say, this could be a long session.'

'You're sure you don't mind?' asked the other, coming back to the desk.

'Not at all.' He glanced at his watch. 'I don't suppose there'll be anyone around to supply us with a cup of coffee, will there?'

'There may be.' A frown gathered between Villiers's eyebrows. He pressed the button on the communicator, waited for a moment, then spoke into it. Flicking the speaker switch with his finger, he said: 'Someone will bring it along in five minutes. They still have a skeleton staff working here until midnight.' Villiers hunched himself forward once more and gave one of his brief, rare smiles that touched the grey eyes behind the glasses more than it did his mouth.

He opened the file and stared down at it for a long moment without speaking. Taking out half a dozen sheets of paper clipped together, he passed them over to Grayson. 'These are the main test results of the static firings we carried out on the engines two weeks ago.' Dryly, he added: 'I think you might find them a little surprising.'

'They appear to be extremely low,' Grayson admitted, glancing swiftly through the first set of figures. 'I suppose there could have been no mistake in the firings?'

'None at all. That was the first conclusion I reached. We've checked and double-checked. Everything was in order, and furthermore — ' He broke off at the knock on the door. 'Come in.' Not until the door had closed again behind the night waitress did Villiers go on with what he had been saying. 'Furthermore, there is that report we received from NASA.'

'I'm afraid I don't recall that one.'

Grayson leaned back, his right fingertips brushing the waistcoat pocket in which the small phial rested. 'Do you think I might see it? Perhaps it will give me something to go on.'

'I'll get it for you.' Villiers got up. 'I think you ought to read it anyway.'

As he moved over to the far side of the room, his back to Grayson, the other moved quickly. There was scarcely any conscious thought in what he did. Fingers gripping the phial tightly, he pulled it swiftly from his pocket, leaning forward as he withdrew the small ground-glass stopper. Varandashky had said that the colourless liquid was absolutely odourless and tasteless, and that it worked within two minutes. He poured it in a thin stream into Villiers's coffee, thrust the empty phial back into his pocket and was leaning back in his chair, fingers intertwined in his lap when the other turned away from the cabinet, the top-secret folder in his hand.

'Some of the mathematics made the going a trifle heavy,' murmured the other as he handed the folder over. 'But I think you'll make out all right. No need to burn the midnight oil though. This problem is going to be with us for some little time in spite of the urgency which the minister has placed on it.'

Grayson put the folder on one side. His answering smile was taut. He felt the quickening of his pulse as the other lifted the cup of coffee and drank it down quickly, anxious to get on with the work in hand without any outside distractions.

The huge building seemed extraordinarily quiet at night. The stillness appeared to build up all around them, accentuated perhaps by the faint murmur of machinery somewhere deep in the basement and the half-muted click of typewriters where the few typists gave the only indication of hidden life in the place. The soft background noise of a car in the distance reached them through the half-open window. It was like the place was some huge animal trying to give the impression that it was asleep, but with one eye open, watchful and alert.

Villiers took the thick file and rifled through it towards the back until he found what he was looking for. He bent the file back so that it lay flat on the desk. Grayson sat quietly in his chair, trying not to allow the coiled impatience within him to radiate across the desk to the other. He could almost feel the red second-hand of the watch on his wrist grinding around the circular dial. Suppose the Reds had been wrong? Suppose this drug they had given him did not have the desired effect? What then? There would undoubtedly be awkward questions asked and answers to be found — satisfactory answers, because this was a culmination of many months of intensive planning. Failure would not be tolerated. He smiled inwardly, wondering what Villiers's reactions would be if he had only the inkling of where he, Grayson, had spent the last two weeks. Would the other try to get to the alarm button, try to summon help — or would he simply sit there, utterly shocked, at the thought that his closest colleague, one of the most trusted men at the establishment, was working for the Russians?

With a sudden movement, Villiers slapped the file shut and pushed it across.

'I think you ought to read through this as soon as possible. It contains all we know, all of our results and — ' He broke off and rubbed a hand across his eyes, screwing them up. 'Strange, I don't seem to . . . '

'Are you all right?' Grayson asked, a look of concern on his face. He got to his feet and moved around the side of the desk towards the other. He was aware of the frenzied beating of his heart, the pounding of the blood in his ears. Even as he reached the other, Villiers slumped forward in his chair, his head falling onto his chest. He would have slipped out of his seat if Grayson hadn't caught him beneath the arm and supported him. Grayson looked briefly down at him, then said sharply: 'Can you hear me, Villiers?'

There was a momentary pause. He was on the point of repeating the question when the other moved slightly. His lips parted and his voice, unnaturally harsh and strident, said: 'I can hear you.'

'Good.' Grayson allowed a brief sigh of relief to issue from his lips. Clearly the drug was everything the Reds had claimed for it. He said briskly: 'I want you to listen to me very carefully. In a few moments we are going to leave the establishment in my car. When we stop at the gate, I shall tell Forbes that you are not feeling well and have decided to leave early. You will answer any questions put to you quite naturally, simply saying that you expect to be back tomorrow morning at the usual time. Do you understand?'

'I understand.' Villiers's blue-grey eyes stared straight ahead of him behind the polished lenses, his face blank. The words came out harshly as if they had somehow been forced upon him, wrung from his lips by some force he neither understood nor was able to control.

'Very well. Now I want you to get me the top-secret files on the new rocket engine, and those concerned with the hardware. I think I'll take this one too.' He picked up the bulky folder from the desk in front of him. 'I'm sure our friends will show some interest in it.'

He watched narrowly as Villiers got to his feet and walked like a man in a trance to the filing cabinet, unlocked one of the drawers, slid it open, took out two files and closed the drawer again, relocking it.

God, Grayson thought, *the Russians must be miles ahead of us in the field of organic research into these new drugs*. Villiers was completely under his control now, as they had prophesied. It was almost as if the other had been hypnotised, only that mental hold he had over the man was far stronger. *Our own people would give their eye teeth for a look at that drug*, he reflected. It was a pity they would never get the chance.

'Let's go,' he said shortly as the other came back with the files. He put on his own jacket and coat and waited while the other did the same, his movements less stiff and jerky than Grayson had expected them to be. It gave him a strange feeling to realise the complete dominance he had over the man's mind. It was as if the other was nothing but a puppet and he was pulling all the strings.

Villiers switched off the lights, behaving just as he would normally do. This was essential. Once the storm broke, as it must inevitably do, there would be enquiries; military intelligence would be brought in, fingerprints taken, men questioned. It was absolutely vital that there should be nothing there to arouse any suspicion. It had to look as if Villiers had simply locked up his office and left in the normal manner. As he reached the door, Grayson recollected one thing, moved back into the room and picked up the two cups of coffee dregs, took them outside and placed them on the trolley at the end of the corridor. They would be picked up in a little while and taken into the kitchen, then washed long before any inquiries could be made.

They met no one in the corridors. Outside in the cool night, Grayson led the way to his car, Villiers following dutifully behind. The top-secret files had been locked away in Villiers's briefcase and Grayson tossed it into the backseat of the car, opened the door for the other to get in, then stood behind the wheel. Three minutes later they were approaching the security block at the gate.

Grayson handed over his own security badge and Villiers's. Bending, as efficient as ever, Forbes peered into the window of the car and stared straight across Grayson at the other. 'You leaving already, Dr. Villiers?' he asked casually.

'I'm afraid that Dr. Villiers isn't feeling too well, Forbes,' Grayson said, forcing evenness into his voice. The urge to push his foot down on the accelerator was almost overpowering. What if something went wrong now? There was a chance that he might be able to get well away before the other could raise the alarm and put anyone on their trail. But that would make it impossible for him to return here and Varandashky had been emphatic that nothing was to point to him; that it was essential he should return to the station at his appointed time.

'Sorry to hear that, sir,' Forbes spoke directly to Villiers. 'Is there anything I can do?'

'No, I shall be quite all right, Forbes. Dr. Grayson will drive me into town. Probably just overwork.'

'Maybe he should have gone on holiday instead of me,' Grayson said with a faint grin. 'Don't worry, Forbes, I'll see that he's all right. Once he gets a breath of fresh air he'll feel better. He must have remained cooped up in that office of his all day.'

'You're probably right, Dr. Grayson. I'd often thought to myself that he does far too much, but he won't listen to anyone. It was only a few months ago that he had all that bother — '

'Yes, yes.' Grayson nodded his head quickly. 'Some other time, Forbes. I think I'd better get him into town. A good night's sleep will do him more good than anything else. Maybe it's better I did come in this evening, otherwise he would have been at it until midnight.'

'There's no doubt about that.' Forbes straightened and moved back a little, and a moment later they were driving through the gate and out onto the country road. Grayson kept the speedometer at around the fifty mark. It was dark now, with only a faint shimmering of starlight, and the headlights dipped and rose almost hypnotically as they drove over the uneven surface of the road. Beside him, Villiers sat like an automaton, eyes fixed straight ahead on the road, no expression whatsoever on his face.

* * *

Thirty-six hours later, in London, the long spell of hot, sultry weather came to an abrupt end in the usual manner. The first warning rumble of thunder echoed from somewhere in the direction of St. James's Park as Steve Carradine climbed into the driving seat of the Mercedes, clicked the gear lever into first and pulled away from the pavement into the stream of traffic. He drove as rapidly as the traffic, the lights and pedestrian crossings would allow. Even now, he could never drive through London without an intense feeling of frustration. He was used to the open country roads of France or Germany, where he could really give the car its head and get from one destination to another in the shortest possible time.

The storm broke almost directly overhead while he was still in the thick of the traffic. Rain slashed at the windscreen and even the moving finger of the wiper did little to take it away. Irritably, Carradine leaned forward in his seat, peering through the film of water which hampered his vision. A vicious flash of lightning winked in the gloom and the roar of the accompanying roll of thunder was like artillery in his ears.

The rain was still coming down in torrents as he pulled into the kerb outside the tall but curiously nondescript building in Regent's Park. He hurried inside the building, the collar of his coat pulled up high around his neck. Two facets of the weather he could not stand, wind and rain — and at that moment there were plenty of both.

Five minutes later, he was in his own room on the third floor. There were several reports on his desk, placed in a neat tray by the ex-Wren who acted as a secretary and the two other agents whose rooms were in this wing of the building on the third floor. Throwing himself down into the red plush chair, he switched on the desk lamp and rifled through the papers, glancing at their contents. He felt oddly restless and disconnected.

He had enjoyed his brief stay in England, especially as the weather had until this morning been extremely fine and warm. But already a sense of inactivity was beginning to grate on his nerves.

The desk work agreed with him only for a couple of weeks at the most between assignments. This time it had gone on for close on three months and he was beginning to feel that, for some reason unknown to himself, the Chief had overlooked him. Carroll, the agent whose room was adjacent to his, had been out of the country, somewhere in the world, for the past five weeks. He didn't know the whereabouts of Fenton; he saw little of the other even when they were both in London at the same time. The Chief did not approve of the men who worked for him knowing too much about each other's affairs. If one of them did have the misfortune to be captured, they would then be able to tell little about the work of their colleagues.

Pulling the topmost file towards him, he told himself that there was only one way to combat boredom and that was to get on with the work in hand and not to feel too damned sorry for himself. The work of the department had to go on no matter how one felt about things. He wondered briefly how he would like the Chief's job. Sitting there in that office somewhere above him, sending out men to all corners of the world, often wondering to himself whether he had signed their death warrants whenever he gave them an assignment, yet never able to go out himself. It took a very special kind of man to hold down a job like that and if anything did go wrong, the repercussions inevitably came back on him. Not that the other's shoulders weren't broad enough to take it, but the strain would sooner or later begin to tell. Carradine was somewhat surprised that it hadn't done so already.

The red telephone on his desk rang stridently. Carradine stared at it for several moments with a sense of surprise. That particular phone was linked directly with the Chief, through the other's secretary. Jerking himself from his surprise, he lifted the receiver.

'Carradine,' he said quietly.

The calm, precise voice of the Chief's secretary sounded in his ears. 'Could you come up, please?'

'The Chief?'

There was a short pause at the other end, then: 'Yes. He wants to see you right away.'

'I'm already on my way.' Carradine replaced the receiver. As he switched off the desk lamp and went out into the corridor, closing the door of the room behind him, he had the odd feeling that perhaps the days of his forced confinement in London were drawing quickly to a close; that maybe the Chief had something in store for him. He did not mind where it was, just so long as it enabled him to get out of this rut into which he had fallen.

The girl seated behind a desk in the small outer office gave him a knowing smile as he went in. It was as if they shared some secret knowledge kept from everyone else. She wore very little make-up, the delicately plucked eyebrows and the faint trace of pale lipstick the only evidence of cosmetics. Yet in spite of that, she was extremely beautiful, exuding an air of warmth and charm that Carradine had rarely seen in other women.

She depressed the switch on the intercom and said quietly: 'Mr. Carradine is here, sir.'

She waited for the metallic 'Send him in at once,' then took her finger away from the switch.

'You've no idea what it is, I suppose?' Carradine said, his voice barely more than a whisper.

She shook her head, still smiling, and motioned towards the door on the far side of the room. 'You'd better ask him.'

The red light was already shining over the Chief's door as Carradine opened it and went inside. The blinds had been opened but outside it was still dark as the storm moved slowly over the city. Carradine walked over to the desk and sat down at the chair facing the Chief. He tried to guess from the expression he saw on the other's face just what lay in store for him, but it was impossible to do so. The other's eyes were hooded under the thick brows.

Finally the other leaned forward, placing his elbows on the desk, fingers touching. 'How are you getting into things? Finding your way around all right?'

Carradine felt his heart sink a little at the other's questions. There was nothing there which indicated he might be receiving another assignment in the near future. Indeed, it sounded as though the Chief intended to keep him on routine duties almost indefinitely.

'Not too badly, sir,' he said finally. 'I must admit the work lacks something.'

'Indeed.' The other's tone was crisp and business-like. There was not the slightest trace of sympathy in his voice. 'I take it that you don't like the routine kind of work we have to do here in London in order to keep you from moving around from one country to another, living off the fat of the land?'

Carradine sat up taut and straight in his chair. He felt a little resentful at the other's remarks. Indeed, it was not the sort of thing the other usually said to his agents. He wondered for a moment if the Chief had got out of bed on the wrong side that morning, or if he had something on his mind which was troubling him more than usual. The other seldom seemed irritated or obviously bothered, whatever happened, and it had never been known for anything to throw him off his stride.

'It's all right.' The other barked a short laugh. 'You don't have to answer that question. I must confess that I never like to keep my more active agents behind a desk any longer than I can possibly help. But things in your particular section have been a trifle quiescent of late and I've had no other alternative. However something *has* just come up which we have to take a look into.' He placed a hand flat on the folder in front of him. 'I'm not sure if this comes into our field of work or not. It's been wished on us by one of the other departments and at the moment I have no option but to go through with it.' He shrugged. 'I have asked for Sir William Cawder to come along. He should be here within the next ten minutes.'

Carradine furrowed his brow. 'Isn't he something to do with the rocket and missile program, sir?'

'That's right. He's deputy head of the project. Exactly why we have had this case dropped into our laps, I couldn't say. I'm rather hoping Sir William will be able to enlighten us when he gets here. At the moment I have only the barest details, I'm afraid. Something to do with a missing scientist from one of their five research stations.'

Carradine raised his brows a little. 'I hope we're not going to have another B. and M. case on our hands. Not that it directly concerned us, but like a stone thrown into a stagnant pool, the ripples tended to move out and touch everyone in the service.'

'You don't have to remind me about that,' murmured the other dryly. 'Because I sincerely hope we don't have to go through that again.' He bent forward to the intercom and depressed the switch. 'Has Sir William Cawder arrived yet?'

'I understand he's just arrived in the building, sir. I'll send him in as soon as he gets here.'

The Chief sat back. He said tightly: 'Don't let Sir William's appearance fool you, Carradine. He may not look usual in the scientific sense, but he has one of the keenest brains in the business. Otherwise he would never have got to where he is now.'

'What are his qualifications, sir?'

'Nuclear physicist. In the top flight too, I understand.'

Carradine said: 'Doesn't it strike you as odd that a nuclear physicist should have been put into a top position in a rocket missile program? I thought they were still using normal chemical fuels in this kind of thing.'

'So did I, until a little while ago. It would appear that we are a little behind the times.' The other waved his hand in an expressive gesture. 'Of course, the work they are engaged on at the moment will probably not bear fruit for a few years yet, but they have already had one or two spectacular successes. Spectacular, that is, in a scientific way. You know how these boys operate. If they get even the slightest indication that their equations are correct, it's a major breakthrough as far as they are concerned. They don't measure success in the same way as we do. We would expect to see a nuclear-powered rocket make a successful soft landing on the moon, probably take off again and get back safely into orbit around the Earth before we could claim any sort of success. But not them. They see a line on a graph, read a certain temperature off a gauge, and that makes their day for them. Anyway, perhaps Sir William can explain their trouble to you better than I can. He should be — ' He broke off as the intercom buzzed briefly. The light winked on over the inside of the door. The Chief pressed a button on top of the desk and a moment later the door opened and Sir William Cawder came in.

Swivelling in his chair, Carradine stared at the other in unveiled surprise. He had not been sure what he had expected, but it had certainly not been this. His mental picture of scientists was of rather untidily dressed individuals who seemed to live in a mental world, only occasionally taking brief glimpses outside of it whenever they were awarded a Nobel prize or something similar.

Sir William Cawder was dressed almost . . . well, foppishly, a large pink carnation adorning his buttonhole, and the silk shirt he wore having a ruffled collar that flowered out around his neck above the string tie. He might have just stepped out of *The Pickwick Papers*, and his manner did little to lessen this image.

The Chief rose to his feet and extended his hand. 'I'm glad you were able to come along, Sir William.'

The other gave a little bow, shook hands, and turned to Carradine as the latter got up. The man had a limp, moist handshake, the kind that Carradine detested, but somehow he managed to keep his feelings from his face as he murmured an appropriate word of greeting, then sat down again.

It was still dark outside although the storm, judging by the lessening of the thunder, was moving away, and the Chief tilted the light on the desk so that it threw its pool of light over the final papers in front of him. There was a moment's silence, broken only by the rattle of the heavy rain against the window pane.

'Now, Sir William. Perhaps you can give us further details of this case. I have had a word with the Home Office. They were able to give me some information, but I must confess that from what I learned from them, this seems to be a straightforward case for the Intelligence Branch. As yet, I fail to see why we should come into it.'

'Then I'll do my best to put you both in the picture. When I'm finished it will be perfectly clear why we have asked you to look into this particular case. As you may be aware, we have five rocket missile research stations in the United Kingdom. Four are what you might call conventional, in that the research carried on there deals with ordinary propellants and the usual type of hardware associated with rocket missiles. The fifth, which is situated between Ashford and Tenterden in Kent, is very different. There we have been carrying out research on the application of nuclear-powered motors to rocketry. Naturally I can't discuss in full what we do there, nor do I think you would want me to do so. We have an excellent team of men working there, the best we have been able to recruit over the past ten or fifteen years.'

'And all of them have been security cleared?' put in Carradine.

Sir William stared at him frostily for a moment as though he had just uttered something so absolutely blasphemous that it did not deserve an answer, then he shrugged his shoulders delicately. 'I think we can honestly say that we have learned our lesson from what has happened in the past. Every man there has been hand-picked and only after the most thorough screening.'

'Yet one of them, at least, may be a traitor,' Carradine persisted, his tone mild.

Sir William eyed him queerly for a second and moistened his lips with the tip of his tongue. 'How do you know that?' he demanded harshly. He turned and looked at the man seated behind the desk.

Now it was Carradine's turn to shrug. He said nonchalantly: 'Call it an inspired guess. It seems to me that unless you had very grave misgivings about one of the men there, you would not have come to us.'

The other grunted noncommittally. 'You're absolutely right, of course.' He glanced at Carradine with new respect. 'We may be barking up the wrong tree entirely, but we can't afford to take the chance of that. The head of our special research section is a man named Charles Villiers, a brilliant man. He's been with us for twelve years, completely trustworthy in every respect. I would have staked my reputation on him. He reported in yesterday as usual. He seemed all right and as far as we know, did his work normally. According to the security guard at the gate, he left with a Dr. John Grayson at nine fifty-three last night. He was a little under the weather. Been working far too hard these past few months. The pressure has been on them from the minister, I'm afraid. But it was nothing they couldn't handle. He was due to come in again this morning at eight-thirty. When he didn't arrive, we checked at his home. His wife and daughter are on holiday in Wales and he was staying alone. We discovered that he had not been there since leaving for the station yesterday morning at his usual time. A check of his office revealed nothing out of the ordinary, except that three very important top-secret files had been taken.'

'Files which dealt with the nuclear side of the work?' Carradine put in.

'I'm afraid so. We started making inquiries immediately this was discovered. Villiers seems to have vanished into thin air. Grayson was probably the last person to see him. He claims he dropped Villiers off at the end of the street in which he lives at about ten-thirty, then drove home, getting in a little before eleven. He seems as surprised as anyone at what has happened.'

'Can the security guard tell you anything?' the Chief asked. 'Was there anything odd about the way in which Villiers acted either during the day or when he left with Grayson?'

'He could add little to what we already know. He did say that Villiers seemed a little uncommunicative, but he put that down to him being a little off-colour. Perhaps I should explain that during the past two years we have had one or two men crack up under the strain. This is hard work and the pressures brought to bear on these men are terrific. There is the continual push from above to keep us not only abreast of the other big powers, but one jump ahead all the time. You can't expect a man to go through this day after day, often taking his work home with him and burning the midnight oil, without something giving.'

After a few moments, the Chief said: 'And you want us to look for this man, Villiers, for you?'

'Yes. And we need those files back before they get into the wrong hands — if they haven't done so already. I don't think I can stress how vital it is to our defence that this should be done as soon as possible.'

2

The Long Scream

The fog through which Charles Villiers seemed to have been swirling for an endless time moved together, began to coagulate, brightened and burned a deep red in his brain. He tried to open his eyes but the moment he did so the sun blinded him, forcing pain back along the optic nerves and into the hollow-ringing emptiness of his skull. He lay absolutely still for several seconds, trying to feel around him with his mind, trusting to the impressions which reached him from various limbs to tell him what he was lying on. It was hard and smooth, and cold. His whole body was cold. Very slowly he forced one eye open and twisted his head a little until the glaring lights slid away from him, hidden by the bridge of his nose. With an effort he drew a gust of air into his lungs. There was a foul taste in his mouth, as if it were stuffed with cotton wool, and his tongue moved rustily between his teeth.

Where in God's name was he? What had happened to him? He struggled desperately to remember, acutely aware that there was a very important reason that he should do so. Tears struggled into his eyes as he forced them to stay open. With a sudden heave, he thrust himself up onto his elbows, retching desperately at the movement. Slowly his eyes cleared; his brain also. Tears came again, half-blinding him as he got to his feet, clinging to the nearby wall for support. There was a painful throbbing at the back of his skull, as if a trip-hammer was beating incessantly at his brain.

After a few minutes he found that he was able to move around without the banging inside his head becoming unbearable. He was in a small, sparsely furnished room. An overhead bulb with a wax-paper shade provided the only light there was, but even so, dim as it was, it still seemed to glare viciously in his eyes. There was a small cracked mirror on one wall and he staggered towards it and peered at his reflection, leaning his weight on his hands. His image stared back at him and for a moment he experienced a sense of shock at what he saw mirrored there. It was almost as if he had aged ten years. The film of black stubble on his face highlighted the sunken cheeks, and the pupils of his eyes seemed dilated to twice their normal size.

How long had he been unconscious? How had he been brought here — and what was more to the point, where was he? Shaking his head, he moved over to the solitary window. It was hung with heavy drapes and he pulled them aside with trembling fingers. There was no welcome sign of daylight on the other side; there was not even night. Instead, his outstretched fingertips encountered the cold, unyielding surface of metal. A thick sheet of steel had been clamped into place over the window.

Villiers squeezed his eyes tightly together for a moment, as though hoping to shut out what he saw, then opened them slowly again; but nothing changed. The smooth satiny surface of the metal, gleaming faintly in the light from the solitary bulb, was still there, a few inches away. He let the heavy drapes fall back into place and turned away, frightened and bewildered. Little snatches of memory were beginning to come back to him like the jumbled bits of a kaleidoscopic pattern in his mind, all twisting and tumbling together, not yet coalescing or making any sense. He had the feeling that the answer was there somewhere, if he could only reach out and grasp it; hold long enough for him to recognise what it was. He forced himself to remember his name. Charles Villiers. Dr. Charles Villiers. He worked at the Rocket Missile establishment near Tenterden, and he was engaged on secret work concerned with the application of nuclear fuels to rocket propulsion, and . . .

He sat down in the high-backed chair at the table and buried his head in his hands. It was all beginning to come back to him now. Grayson had come to see him last night — was it last night, or the night before? They had been going over the latest filing results when he had felt ill. After that he recalled nothing.

Opening his fingers, he peered through them at the plain table. Why had he been brought here? There was no longer any doubt in his mind that he had been drugged and that, he realised with a faint thrill of horror, could mean only one thing.

Grayson! But why? For the life of him, he could imagine no earthly reason why the other should do anything like this. There had never been any animosity between the two of them. They had always worked together in the closest harmony. They had never been what one would call close friends, because Grayson was not really the kind of man who made friends easily; a lone wolf who preferred to be left alone to do his work. He shook his head. The movement hurt and the throbbing pain at the back of his neck came back.

Somehow, he had to get out of there. He heaved himself to his feet and went over to the door, conquering the dizziness that went through him. He was sweating profusely by the time he got to the door and tried to open it, but discovered there was no handle. For a long moment he stared down at the place where the handle ought to have been, feeling the fear wash up again inside him, now more strongly than before. It was impossible for him to help himself. In the face of this blankness in his mind, which would not allow him even a glimpse into what had happened to him, he became little more than a trapped animal. He beat at the unyielding panels of the door until his hands were raw and bleeding, until there was no further strength left in his body, until a scream tried to force its way through his clamped, tight teeth and came out as no more than a frightened whimper of sound.

* * *

Carradine had not expected it to be so easy. So far, in spite of the fact that there was still a good hour of daylight left, there had been no sign that the driver of the car in front of him had any suspicion that he was being followed. He had had to do some fast motoring once they had left Ashford behind, and the road had become more and more deserted. But he was not too worried now. If Grayson was suspicious, he would give some sign of it in time for him to change his plans a little.

Carradine was still not sure in his own mind what he was going to gain by following Grayson. But the other was the only slender lead he had and if anyone was going to make the wrong move, he was determined that it should be the other. With all of his past experience in this sort of business, he had developed a curious sixth sense about people. There had, he decided, been something distinctly phoney about the other which he had noticed when he had talked with him that morning.

There was, of course, the possibility that Villiers had suddenly thrown over the traces and had a nervous breakdown, and the disappearance of the top-secret files was nothing more than a coincidence. Sir William had freely admitted that certain top officials at the research station sometimes took such files away with them, although they had to be checked back the following morning with the security personnel on the site. The one thing which worried him on this point was that Villiers had apparently not mentioned to anyone that he intended taking these files with him that evening as he was supposed to do, and the other was too experienced a man to forget the regulations. That left only two possibilities: either Villiers was a traitor and had gone over to the Reds — or he was innocent and the victim of a plot to get him out of the country by force. There was no doubt that the Russians would give anything to have the vital knowledge which Villiers had tucked away in his mind. If the former alternative was correct, then the chances were that Villiers was already out of the country and perhaps beyond their reach. But if he were not a traitor, then that was a very different kettle of fish. It meant that a long finger of suspicion was pointing directly at the man who had last seen him alive; the man who had the best opportunity of spiriting Villiers and those precious files past the noses of the security men at the entrance of the Missile Establishment. John Grayson.

Why not? Of course, he was only acting on a hunch. He had no positive proof of this. He smiled at the thought which flashed through his mind. This was, in all probability, the reason why Sir William had placed this case in their lap and not brought in the Home Office or the civil police. They would be unable to do anything; would have their hands tied before they could really act. Whereas if there was to be any rough stuff, then he would not hesitate to carry it out. If the only way to wring information from Grayson was to do it by means of physical violence, then he would resort to it without any qualms.

There was still the question of how Grayson had succeeded in getting Villiers to go with him so docilely. He had the feeling that there had been no question of Grayson holding a gun on the other while he drove him out of the establishment. Such a crude method would not appeal to these men. They would have used something far more refined, far less capable of being detected. Villiers would have only to have said something to expose Grayson when they had halted at the security block. He knit his brows in sudden concentration. It had to be something else.

A drug of some kind? It was possible. He did not doubt that Grayson would have had an opportunity to administer it. From what he had been told, the two men had been served with coffee about half an hour after Grayson had arrived there. He was still thinking of this, driving completely relaxed, playing with his thoughts, turning the various theories over in his mind, filling in the details wherever possible, when he suddenly realised that the black limousine ahead of him had slowed and was now moving forward at a crawl. Carradine woke up from his daydreaming. Swiftly, he lifted his foot off the accelerator and eased it down gently on the brake. It was possible that the other had caught sight of him in the mirror and had become suspicious of a car following him all this way, keeping essentially the constant distance, and had slowed to give him the chance to draw level and then overtake.

Smiling grimly, Carradine pressed more firmly on the brake. A moment later he was out of sight of the other below a long, sloping rise. Easing the car gently forward, he caught a glimpse of the other rounding a sharp bend perhaps half a mile ahead. Here, there was a thick grove of trees that grew all the way down to the road, culminating in a high grassy bank, looming perhaps five feet above the road.

Carradine drove on, his face lined in thought. There was something very fishy here, although at the moment he wasn't sure what it was. He approached the bend slowly, not wanting to come upon the other without warning if Grayson had stopped and was waiting for him. As it was, he was just creeping around the corner when he came upon the limousine. It was parked some three hundred yards along the road, the nearside wheels drawn onto the grassy verge. Ramming his foot down hard on the brake, Carradine stopped, turned his head and looked about him. He saw a small opening which led into a nearby field and backed the Mercedes into it.

Opening the glove compartment, he took out a small but powerful pair of binoculars, got out and walked quickly to the end of the opening, keeping the high hedge between himself and the distant car. Grayson was seated at the wheel of the limousine, fingers idly drumming on it, occasionally turning his head to look about him, scanning the road behind him as well as that in front.

Now what the devil was he waiting for here? Could Villiers be somewhere around? It seemed highly unlikely, but not completely out of the question. Once or twice, the other checked the watch on his wrist. He seemed impatient, afraid, anxious to be on his way again before anyone came along.

Carradine watched warily. His first impression had been that this was a post office for Grayson, where he would pick up further instructions or payment for services rendered. Now it seemed almost certain that this was not the case. Then a moment later there was a sudden movement at the very edge of his vision. He turned his head swiftly, pushing the lenses of the binoculars to his eyes, adjusting the focusing screw slightly to bring the scene into almost blinding clarity. It was dim in the undergrowth that grew thickly along the trunks of the trees, but a moment later he saw the tall shape of a man come out of the brush, climb lithely over the top of the steep bank and run towards the car. There was a moment of rapid conversation, then the man got into the car beside Grayson. There was the distant roar of the engine accelerating, the squeal of tyres on the road and then the car was moving off again, heading away in a rapid start, leaving a very slowly dissipating cloud of blue smoke from the exhaust hanging in the air. Carradine cautiously watched the car until it disappeared, then ran back to the Mercedes and slid in behind the wheel.

Grayson kept to the A20 for several miles, passing through Sellindge with Carradine less than half a mile behind him. By now it was almost dark and

Carradine was forced to keep the red rear lights of the other car in view, closing up a little so that he would not lose him somewhere along the road into Folkestone. There were, he recalled, several side roads into which the other could turn before they reached the coast. Somehow, he did not expect Grayson to head into Folkestone and he was not surprised when, approaching the roundabout at the junction of the A20 and the A261, he saw the twin red lights blink once and then vanish. He slowed instinctively, and drove in first gear as he strained his eyes to pick up the other once more. Fortunately there was little traffic on the road, and a few moments later he sighted the rear lights once more, heading along the B2068 to the south.

Now where was the other going? As far as Carradine knew, the secondary road led virtually nowhere. Twenty minutes later, with the red lights still glinting tantalisingly in front of him, showing no sign of slowing or stopping, they reached the Royal Military Road, crossed it and headed into Romney Marsh. Here there was such a maze of small roads that Carradine reached a sudden decision, took a chance and switched off his lights, moving up close to the other before he lost the scent. They were approaching the small village of Burmarsh now and, although there was a reddish glow low on the western horizon, it gave light only on the skyline, and Carradine had to do some very skilful motoring to prevent himself from running into trouble. The road was narrow, winding and twisting so that it was almost impossible to pick out the bends until he was right on top of them. The road was badly cambered and he took no chances.

Burmarsh showed up directly ahead, a few lights gleaming yellow in the windows. Leaning forward, Carradine watched the red lights in front of him, saw the brake lights come on and slowed instinctively. Was this the end of the line? Why had Grayson come here; and why the secrecy surrounding his meeting with this other man, unless he was implicated in the disappearance of Charles Villiers and those top-secret files?

* * *

The light from the single overhead bulb still shone dimly in the small room. Faint though it was, there seemed to be no shadows anywhere, even in the corners where they would be expected. Villiers opened his eyes, looked about him blankly for a moment, then pushed himself to his knees, kneeling there swaying for a moment. He felt oddly sick and there was a cold slickness of sweat on his face, trickling down his cheeks and dripping from his chin. He closed his eyes instinctively, squeezing them shut, and waited.

Why in God's name was he feeling like this? Surely the coffee hadn't had this effect on him. There had been nothing wrong with the taste of it and, after all, Grayson had taken some and he seemed to have fared all right, otherwise . . .

He stared about him blankly. Where was Grayson? He wiped the back of his sleeve over his face and stared down at the dark, wet stain where the perspiration had soaked into the cloth. What the hell was this all about? He tried to orientate himself and scrambled to his feet. Then sickness overcame him and he was forced to stagger quickly to the basin in one corner of the room where he was violently ill. Turning on the tap, he stepped back and looked at himself in the dusty, cracked mirror. His fingers touched the black stubble on his chin wonderingly.

What had happened? He remembered talking with Grayson in his office. They had been discussing the latest test results with the new engines. That was it. For some reason, Grayson had come in two days earlier than he was due back and had agreed to talk things over with him, so that he could get to grips with the problem when he returned to his work at the beginning of the week.

Moving back into the middle of the room, he felt the nails of his fingers dig deeply into the flesh of his palms. There was something dreadfully wrong here, something really frightening and —

There came a sudden click and the door without a handle was pushed open. He felt a sudden sharp rise of apprehensive fear as someone came into the room, then relaxed a little as he saw who it was.

'John! For God's sake, what's going on here?'

Grayson smiled cheerfully. He stood on one side and another man came into the room with him. Villiers narrowed his eyes as he stared at the other. The man was a complete stranger to him. He was tall and broadly built, with a wide, chunky face and dark eyes set deep in folds of flesh. It was a big, crag-like face with strong bones under the flesh and a forward-jutting chin. The thick lips formed a sullen mouth which Villiers guessed could so easily fall into a cruel smile.

'I'm sorry we had to inconvenience you in this way, Charles,' Grayson said, speaking casually. He closed the door behind him and locked it. 'Unfortunately, it was very necessary.'

'What do you mean?' Villiers looked at him curiously. There was a sudden dryness in his mouth. 'What is all this about?'

Grayson smiled. 'It would seem that fate has decided that you are worth far more to my friends than you are to the

British government. It would really surprise you to know how much your work is appreciated in countries other than this.' The other sat down in one of the chairs, crossed his legs and regarded Villiers calmly. He went on in a relaxed, conversational tone. 'It will be quite obvious to you that certain people will pay a large sum of money to obtain the information we possess. The difference between you and I is that whereas you have strong so-called principles, I do not feel hidebound by such things. I find them far too restrictive.' He shrugged his shoulders eloquently. 'Naturally I am grateful to the British government for giving me the opportunity of working in this particular field of research, which has always been very close to my own heart. But you must admit yourself that the amount of funds which they allocate to us is meagre considering the importance of the work we do.'

'So you've decided to sell that information to the enemy,' Villiers said grimly. 'I suppose I should have known.'

Grayson shook his head admonishingly.

'Not the enemy, Charles. Not since the Crimean War have the Russians been our enemies. They were our allies in the last war and very few people realise how many of them died so that we had the chance to build up our own forces for the Normandy invasion.'

'I'm not interested in that,' Villiers said harshly. He still felt sick deep in the bottom of his stomach, but forced the sensation down with a supreme effort. 'All that concerns me is that you have betrayed our secrets to the enemy. Yes,' he went on thinly, 'the enemy. Because that is what they are. Do you think for one minute that you will ever succeed in getting out of their clutches now? Do you think they will go on paying you indefinitely unless you continue to provide them with the information they want? And when they decide that you are of no further use to them, they'll have you killed without the slightest compunction.'

Grayson looked gravely at him. 'You're a stupid fool, Charles,' he said equably. 'You know nothing of the way they work. I have done all that they have asked of me. In three days I shall be in the Soviet Union, where I shall have a department of my own in one of their research laboratories, and unlimited funds to do the work I wish to do.' He paused, pursed his lips and stared down at his interlaced fingers for a moment. 'Now if you only saw sense, I could arrange it so that you had the same chance. I'm quite sure that — '

'Save your breath, Grayson.' There was naked scorn in the other's tone. 'I wouldn't work for them if they gave me all the money in Russia.'

'Then you are making a very big mistake.' Grayson took out a cigarette, flicked the wheel of his lighter and blew smoke into the air, tilting his head back and watching the smoke curl up to the low ceiling. 'Because in that case, you must realise that we cannot allow you to give away what you know about us. There will be no trouble, I assure you. Colonel Varandashky here is very adept at carrying out these things with no hitches. It is never difficult to ensure that someone vanishes without trace. There have been more than two hundred unsolved cases in Britain alone of people disappearing into thin air and never being found. Many of them are the direct result of men such as the Colonel here. The police will keep an open file on the case as they have on all of the others, but without a body . . . ' He shrugged his shoulders once more and left the remainder of his sentence unsaid but the threat, the menace in his meaning, was more eloquent than if he had spoken it out loud.

'And the top-secret files? I suppose you have them too?'

'They are quite safe, I assure you. I personally will see to it that they are delivered into the right hands.' Grayson drew deeply on the cigarette, the tip waxing and waning redly.

Villiers, with an effort, forced himself to think clearly. He was no fool. He knew that Grayson meant every word he said; that the other had not been lying when he had claimed that he would be able to get out of England without being spotted by the authorities. Evidently this thing had been very carefully planned. The security regulations at the missile station had been tightened considerably during the past few months. For Grayson to have fooled them all at that time was a sure indication of how good this organisation was. He felt a little shiver go through him. 'You are the one making the mistake,' he said harshly. 'You're underestimating the resources of the authorities here. How can you be so sure that they aren't on to you right now, even closing in on this place, wherever it is?'

'Oh they are making their usual routine enquiries,' said the other, making a derogatory motion with his arm. 'There were some men down at the establishment this morning asking the usual questions. They may even suspect me of having had a part in your disappearance, but whether that is so or not is a matter of complete indifference to me. By the time they get around to taking any action, we shall be inside Soviet territory and then, of course, we shall both have disappeared without trace.'

Villiers stood quite still for a long

moment, staring down at the other's impassive face. For a long time he had forgotten the bulky figure of the Russian — for such he now knew the other to be — standing near the locked door. Quite suddenly, there seemed to be nothing fantastic about what the other was saying. The idea of him being spirited away like this under the very noses of the British authorities was bizarre only in the magnitude of the operation. It was quite evident that he was in the hands of a vast, powerful, worldwide organisation which specialised in this sort of thing; the kidnapping of important men, the spiriting of them away behind the Iron Curtain.

He felt suddenly tired. 'Just how do you propose to get at the information locked away in my mind?' he asked. 'The usual Gestapo methods?'

Grayson smiled, but it was merely a twitching of his lips.

'But of course not. We shall simply use the same method as I did when I got you away from the establishment under the very noses of the security guards. It was really childishly simple.'

'You drugged my coffee.'

'Ah yes, but a very special kind of drug,' enthused Grayson. 'One which is quite unknown to British scientists. You still don't seem to have got the full picture. You've been so indoctrinated with the idea that the Reds are years behind us in research, but nothing could be further from the truth. They're good — really good. There's nothing better than some of the discoveries they've made. This drug works within two minutes, on anyone, and in that time the victim is completely under one's control. Just like hypnotism, Charles, only twice as effective and sure, and far stronger. You walked out to my car last night and we spoke to Forbes at the security gate, yet you know nothing of it, nothing at all. The last you will have remembered, until the effects of the drug wore off sometime today, will be talking to me in your office, just before you drank your coffee.'

Once more the cold shiver of fear raced along Villiers's spine, but this time it was because he knew that the other was speaking the truth.

Grayson wiped the breezy expression off his grinning face. He got to his feet, stubbed out the butt of his cigarette in the empty saucer on the table and braced his legs. Glancing down at the watch on his wrist, he said quietly: 'Well, I think it's time we were moving. As you can guess, everything had to be planned and timed to the second. I trust that you are not going to try anything foolish and attempt to escape. Really you have no choice. Either you come along with us without any trouble, or we repeat the performance of last night. It's entirely up to you.'

Villiers took one look at the pitiless face, glanced obliquely at the man leaning against the wall near the door and made his decision. He shrugged resignedly.

Grayson nodded. 'Now you are showing sense, Charles.' There was a faint beat of sarcasm in his voice. 'Really it is much better this way. And who knows; once we get to our destination and you can see for yourself the facilities which are offered to men such as ourselves, you may change your mind.'

'Never!' Villiers spat the single word through tightly clenched teeth. He moved over to the door as Grayson came forward. The Russian pushed himself away from the wall. His deadpan eyes never left Villiers's face as he unlocked the door and opened it, motioning him to precede him.

Cold air sighed around Villiers as he stepped outside. There was a short flight of stone steps and a weed-overgrown path, and off in the distance a cluster of houses showed up faintly on the skyline, one or two of the windows filled with yellow light. He looked about him as he climbed the steps. The cold night air did more to clear his head than a dousing with cold water would have done. Somewhere in the distance, there was the faint booming whistle of a ship. So they were not very far from the coast. But how far? he wondered. He knew only too well that at night, with sounds carrying well, hearing was the most deceptive of the senses.

The tall Russian came at his back. To ensure that he did not forget to do everything he was told, he felt something hard dig into the small of his back and knew it was the barrel of a gun. The door of the building clicked shut behind them. It was impossible to know whether Grayson had switched off the light inside before coming out. Villiers remembered that thick sheet of metal over the window and knew that not a solitary chink of light would ever show through that.

Grayson's feet sounded on the stone steps. He heard the other utter a soft curse as he stumbled in the darkness.

'Keep moving, my friend,' grunted the Russian gutturally. The gun barrel jabbed more firmly into his back. Villiers winced instinctively. For the first time he realised that the other spoke English. It came as a momentary surprise to him. Back in that dingy room, it had been Grayson who had done all the talking.

Ahead of them was a wide stretch of open ground dotted with clumps of tough grass and short, stunted bushes. There was an orchard near a broken-down wall fifty yards or so to the right, and a little to his left he noticed a narrow road that ran through the centre of the village. There was a sharp smell of the sea in his nostrils; a wet, salty smell that tingled at the back of his throat.

The ground underfoot was slippery and treacherous, with patches of mould and damp leaves. Villiers tensed. Just beyond the wall, a little way off the road, he caught a glimpse of the car that stood waiting for them, a car with no light showing. In a few minutes he would be bundled inside it and they would be driving away to a destination so far from England that he would be buried there and lost forever. That was the damnable part of this whole business. That and the feeling of utter helplessness, knowing that whether or not he wanted to aid these people, he would have to do so in the end.

A few more seconds; a few more yards.

3

Such Men Are Dangerous

In the darkness it was difficult to distinguish the three figures that came out of the low-roofed building. Carradine, the Luger held uncertainly in his hand, crouched down in the wet grass just behind the low stone wall. It was only as the trio drew level with him, perhaps twenty feet away, that he recognised Grayson walking in the rear. The man who lumbered forward immediately in front of him was the tall, solidly-built man he had seen getting into the car along the road from Ashford.

That left only the man who walked hesitantly in the lead. The chances were that it was Villiers, the missing physicist. Carradine shook himself. Somehow he had to get the other away from the two men with him, but that was not going to be easy in the darkness and with what looked suspiciously like a gun or a knife pressed into the middle of Villiers's back. At the moment he could not risk getting off even one shot at the man holding the weapon. Even in the split second that it took the bullet to travel the twenty feet or so, the other could squeeze the trigger and send a bullet into Villiers's spine. He felt tense and helpless.

Easing his way forward, feeling the tall grass brush his knees, he moved along the side of the wall. The black limousine was parked less than thirty feet away, by the side of the small farm lane that led off the village road. No light showed and it was little more than a vague patch of shadow even at that distance.

There was only one chance, he decided. Once the men reached the stone wall they would be forced to separate a little to get over it, even where it was broken in one place. Carradine looked along the twenty feet or so of path that led along the wall. He picked out the places where he could put his feet without making any sound, then he eased his way out from behind the wall and ran, body bent almost double. He ran along the edge of the wall so close that his right elbow scraped along it in places, then got to the spot he had chosen and crouched there, forcing the breath slowly through his parted teeth, poised like a panther in the darkness. He heard the rustle of feet. Someone cursed softly under their breath.

Then Villiers appeared less than three feet away. His head and shoulders loomed over the crenellated top of the walls where several of the pieces of stone had fallen away.

'Over,' grunted the man behind him.

Carradine saw Villiers stiffen a little, then swing his leg over the broken portion of the wall. A few moments later he had clambered over and was standing with his back to Carradine, staring off into the darkness towards the waiting car. Carradine tensed himself, every muscle poised. He did not want to have to use the gun if he could help it. Far better to take these two men alive and turn them over to R. Branch for interrogation. There was little doubt that they would be able to tell the service quite a lot, and even less doubt that they would do so. He knew little of the ways of the men of R. Branch, but he had seen some of their results and knew that their methods, whatever they were, invariably paid off.

Another leg swung over the wall, almost within reach of Carradine's hand. He heard the scrape of the toecaps on the rough stone surface and the sudden grunt as the man, straining to keep upright so that he might keep the gun in his hand levelled on Villiers, eased his way over the wall. The shoe touched the grass in front of him, knee bent a little to take the weight of the body coming over behind it.

Carradine felt his muscles coil as he waited. The man slid over, straightened up and turned to move after Villiers. In a violent surge of movement, Carradine rose, throwing himself forward, the butt of the pistol in his hand striking down at the back of the big man's neck. He had planned to knock the other out, then turn on Grayson, but some hidden instinct seemed to warn the big man of his danger. He swung sharply and the heavy butt of the gun caught him on the shoulder blade, knocking him forward, off balance, but not doing any real damage. He heard the sudden yell that the other gave, and turned his head instinctively as Grayson flung himself over the top of the wall at him. A flailing hand caught him on the side of the head, half-stunning him. Somehow he still retained his grip on the gun as he fell sideways.

Grayson was shouting wildly now and the big man had turned, bringing round the hand holding the gun, levelling it at Carradine as he lay in the wet grass. Half on his back, Carradine kicked out wildly and felt his toe connect with the other's leg just below the knee. The man staggered back just as he pulled the trigger. There was a soft, vicious plop of a silencer and the bullet hummed within an inch of Carradine's head, burying itself in the ground immediately behind him.

Carradine desperately struggled to turn the gun in his hand. There would be no refined method here. He had to kill these two men before they finished him. He did not know whether Grayson was armed and his first concern was for the man with the gun. He saw the other struggle upright, holding on to the wall with one hand to keep his balance. He was breathing heavily, his eyes glaring redly in the shadow of his face. He came forward very slowly, gripping the heavy gun with the ugly silencer screwed onto the barrel tightly in his right hand.

Desperately, savagely, Carradine lifted the gun, knowing that he would be seconds too late. He could make out the hatred on the glaring face, the eyes shining in the dimness. Then, without warning, the man uttered a loud, harsh cry of pain, dropped the gun and clutched at his wrist. A few feet away, Villiers lifted the heavy piece of wood he had used to smash the other's wrist high over his head. Carradine's scrabbling legs got a hold under him in the slippery dirt. He heaved himself to his knees. Grayson swung a booted foot at him and caught him on the thigh, sending a sharp spasm of agony lancing through his leg. As he knelt there, he was aware of the sound of running feet in the distance.

With an effort, he forced his sight

through his blurred vision. The big man was racing for the waiting car. Carradine staggered upright. For the moment, he had forgotten about Grayson. It crossed his mind that the other would really know very little about this enemy organisation, whereas the big man probably knew a lot. He was the more important and possible the more dangerous of the two at the moment.

The other had reached the car and wrenched the door open even as Carradine got to his feet. He could just make out the other's dark shape as the man flung himself behind the wheel and twisted the ignition key in the starter. The engine roared, bursting into instant life. The headlights came on, highlighting the trees and the white stone wall. The man leaned forward and picked up something from the seat beside him.

Carradine never quite knew what saved his life at that moment. Perhaps it was an inbred knowledge of how these people operated, and knowledge born of several years of working against them. But, as the other twisted suddenly in the driving seat, he hurled himself forward face-downward on the soft earth, his head pulled well into the crook of his arms, face pressed into the earth.

Even as he hit the ground, the small bomb exploded less than ten feet away. Steel splinters spread through the air over his head, humming through the darkness around him. Carradine twisted over, pushing himself onto one elbow as the car moved, tyres spinning for a moment as they failed to grip the soft, slippery soil. Then the limousine was moving, forcing its way off the grassy verge and onto the cinder track. It gathered speed swiftly. Aiming sharply, he sent two shots after it as it vanished into the darkness, reached the intersection with the village road and turned out of sight.

With an effort he pushed himself to his feet, gasping air down into his heaving lungs. Thrusting the gun into his belt, he walked over to the two men near the wall. Grayson was on his knees, head and shoulders resting against the hard, rough surface of the wall. Villiers was staring helplessly down at him, his face working, lips twisting but no sound coming out.

'What happened to him?' Carradine asked tersely. He caught hold of Villiers's arm, fingers biting into it roughly. He could see the other was almost on the verge of hysteria. That had to be stopped at all costs. There were questions he needed answered and Villiers was the only man who could supply the answers at that time.

'I think he's hurt,' said the other in a low, hushed tone. 'What in God's name was that explosion?'

'Some kind of bomb or grenade he had ready, just in case of trouble,' Carradine said. He bent, pulled Grayson's thick coat open, and drew back the jacket and shirt. There was a thin trickle of blood on the man's chest oozing from a gash high in the right shoulder. Evidently he had got in the way of a piece of flying shrapnel from that bomb. It was a sort of poetic justice, he thought grimly. It was going to hurt like hell, but it would not be fatal, although temporarily incapacitating.

'We'll get him to a hospital,' he said, straightening up again. 'It looks worse than it really is. Then we'll have to question him.' He eyed Villiers closely. 'He was in this plot with them, wasn't he?'

'Yes.' Villiers spoke in a low whisper. 'They were going to take me with them. Back to somewhere in Russia, he said. I'm not sure whether he meant it.'

'Don't fool yourself,' Carradine said grimly. 'Take my word for it. He meant every word of it. We are up against a tremendous organisation scattered throughout Britain and Europe. Let's just say we were damnably lucky this time.'

Bending over the groaning man, he pulled him to his feet and between them they managed to get him back to Carradine's car.

* * *

The elevator stopped. Carradine got out and made his way quickly to the room at the end of the corridor. This time there was no banter with the smiling secretary in the outer office. The air of urgent mystery seemed to pervade the atmosphere, even here. Carradine had been aware of it from the moment he had received the call to go up to the chief's room at once. It had been a summons he had expected ever since that affair at the rocket missile station almost a week before.

The chief's face was cold and blank as Carradine walked in and took a seat in front of the other. There was a single file lying on the highly polished surface in front of him. Carradine stared down at it for a moment, almost subconsciously reading the words which were printed on it, upside-down as far as he was concerned. There was a red top-secret star in the upper right-hand corner and beneath it, in capital letters: PORTUGESE STATION, SUSPECTED CONTACT — IVAN VARANDASHKY.

Carradine knitted his brows in thought. Now who on earth was Ivan Varandashky? And what had he to do with the Portuguese station? As far as Carradine was aware, they had never had any real trouble in Portugal. Naturally the service had a small station there, just to keep an eye on things. Portugal had been Britain's ally for far longer than any other European country. It had been a matter of pride with the Portuguese. There had hadn't been a war between the two countries for many centuries.

The chief drew the folder towards him and opened the first page, glancing down at the contents. 'That was an excellent piece of work you did a week ago, Carradine. I must confess that the success of it surprised even me. The minister is extremely pleased.'

'It was nothing more than a hunch, sir,' Carradine said, leaning back. What did the other have on his mind now? he wondered tensely. It was not like him to pass out compliments of this nature unless there was something really nasty and sticky coming up.

'Nevertheless, you carried it through very well. This other man with Grayson got away. That was unfortunate, but we can't have everything, I suppose. Not all at once, that is.'

'Do we know where he is then, sir?' Carradine asked.

The other shook his head. 'I'm afraid

he must have slipped out of the country.' His voice was quiet, dangerous. 'Do you have any final thoughts about this affair?'

Carradine pursed his lips. 'None, sir.' He kept his eyes on the desk in front of him. 'But surely either Grayson or Villiers has talked?'

The Chief nodded. 'Villiers knows very little, I'm afraid. He did not even know where he was kept. Undoubtedly they used some kind of drug on him, one our men would like to get their hands on. Apparently it places the victim in some form of hypnotic trance. He will implicitly obey any command given to him, acting outwardly in quite a natural manner. We never deemed that their chemists had got such a tremendous lead in the synthesis of these drugs. As you can imagine, the Americans are also keenly interested in this aspect of the case.'

'I can well imagine that,' Carradine said dryly. He knew that the other had not called him in here just to talk about the drug which had been used on Villiers. There was something far more to it than that.

After a moment's pause, the other tapped the file in front of him with a blunt forefinger. 'I've decided to put you onto this assignment, Carradine,' he said softly. 'The report on John Grayson will be here in a little while. I want to go through it with you. I've seen a little of what they learned from him. It makes very interesting reading.'

'Somehow I didn't think he would be able to give us very much information of importance that we don't know already.'

The heavy brows lifted a little and there was a faint smile on the other's lips. 'It isn't exactly the information he can give us, so much as the chance of putting tiny isolated pieces of news together and forming a coherent picture for the first time. By the time we have it all, I think there should be enough of it for you to know just what you'll be up against.'

'I had a feeling that the Villiers case wasn't finished when we got him back,' Carradine said.

The other ignored the comment. 'This wasn't only an isolated instance. There have been several similar cases during the past six or seven years. Important men have gone missing, leaving no trace, no clue. We don't doubt that they were spirited away out of the country and under our very noses. So far we've had no clue as to the route they take. Now we have this, all of it built up during the past few days, mostly from what we've managed to wring out of Grayson.' He smiled thinly. 'Unless I'm very much mistaken, our friends in Redland are going to be very angry with Colonel Varandashky.'

Carradine allowed his glance to drop towards the file. That had been the name on it. To his left a light winked on the intercom. The other leaned over and pressed down a switch.

'Yes?'

'The report on Dr. Grayson, sir.'

'Good. Bring it in right away, please.'

The Chief's eyes were narrowed a little as he sat back and watched the door leading into the outer office. It opened a moment later and his secretary came in, placed the report on his desk and went out again, closing the door gently behind her.

'We went to a great deal of trouble to get this.' The other tapped it significantly with his forefinger. 'I sincerely hope that it's worth it.'

'Do they have any idea of the nature of the drug used on Villiers?'

'Nothing, I'm afraid. Varandashky gave it to Grayson, together with the instructions for its use. That's all we know about it. He took the precaution of getting rid of the phial, and the coffee cup was washed by the waitress at the establishment within an hour of those two men leaving. We're still utterly in the dark there, I'm afraid.'

'Just who is this man Varandashky? I don't think I've come up against him so far.'

'You haven't,' said the other shortly. 'He's an extremely dangerous man. He gave us some trouble about three years ago. We lost four of our best men there and he still managed to slip through our fingers. It would be quite a feather in our cap if we could lay him by the heels.'

Carradine nodded his head very slowly in gradual understanding. 'And being one of their top men, you feel he may be operating in Portugal?'

The bushy brows went up a further millimetre, then the other smiled. 'I would go even further than that and say we are ninety-nine percent certain that he operates from inside Portugal.'

'But why Portugal, sir? Surely of all the European countries, it would be the last on their list of forward bases?'

'Do you really think so? Our station in Portugal is very small. There has been no trouble, barring a few minor incidents, ever since it was set up there before the war. Working as we do in this department on a shoestring, we have not seen the necessity of enlarging the station. Somehow I doubt if this has escaped the eyes of our friends.'

'So they move in there in force.' Carradine rubbed a finger down the side of his nose. 'But what do they hope to gain? I mean, surely there is nothing in Portugal for them. If they wanted to keep an eye on NATO bases and exercises they could do it far more easily and efficiently from one of the other countries, especially

Britain or the Scandinavian area. So there has to be something more.'

'Exactly,' said the other heavily. He rifled through the papers in the report. 'There has to be something more. Whatever it is — and as yet we know very little — it is of vital importance that we should know of it as soon as possible. They would not waste a man of Varandashky's abilities on a task of secondary importance. This is big, Carradine, really big. And the fact that it is happening on our own doorstep makes it all the more vital that we know of it.' His mouth tightened into a faint smile. 'We don't want another Cuba, you know.'

'And our men in Portugal, sir?' Carradine interjected. 'Who is head of the station there?'

'A man called Corella. Excellent man. He's been there since early in the war. Only thing about him is that he's a little frustrated now. I think he enjoyed the job at first, maybe hoped that Portugal might enter the war and he would see a little more action. But since it's a very quiet station, he's seen little or nothing. I often feel he resents this, although he would never admit it to anyone.' He waved his hand expressively. 'I'd drop this case into his lap, but he's been out of these things for so long it may be asking for trouble. Anyway, with the big guns such as Varandashky around, I think it calls for one of my best men. If they can throw a man like that at us, then I'm dammed sure I can toss one right back at them.' His piercing gaze seemed to bore right through Carradine.

'Meaning me?' Carradine tried to keep the note of eagerness out of his voice. After losing that man back there in Burmarsh, he was more than anxious to get to grips with him again, make sure that he did not repeat the performance of underestimating him.

'Meaning you,' the chief said. 'You'd better take this and read it from cover to cover. Also the file on this case. It ought to give you enough background information to let you know what you'll be running into when you get to Portugal.'

Carradine reached across and picked up the two files. He looked directly into the other's eyes. He knew perfectly well why he was getting this assignment. He was one of the few men in the service who had seen Varandashky, even though it had been only a fleeting glimpse in the dark; and he had been responsible for him getting away. Now he was getting another chance. He got to his feet, tucking the two files under his arm. The man behind the desk glanced up at him as he moved away.

'Just one more thing, Carradine. Like I said, we don't know what is going on out there and don't you go jumping in with both feet, underestimating these men, simply because on the face of it nothing can possibly be happening in Portugal.'

Carradine felt a wave of resentment burn through him, then he thrust it away quickly. The chief was possibly quite right in this criticism of him. In the past, he had sometimes tended to disregard caution and just go in, leading with his chin. It had often got him into bad trouble.

'I'll do my best, sir.'

'Good. I'm sure you will, otherwise I wouldn't let you have this particular assignment.' It was not too difficult for the chief to read the look of growing tension and excitement in Carradine's eyes. He had seen that there on several previous occasions when he had sent this man out to some remote corner of the world, dicing with death as few men did. Sitting back in his chair, he sighed a little, placed the tips of his fingers together and said very softly: 'There is a plane leaving for Lisbon tomorrow afternoon. I have already made a reservation for you.'

'I'll be on it, sir.' He turned and walked swiftly out of the room.

⋆ ⋆ ⋆

The next day Carradine stood against the wide, curving glass window at the airport and watched the airliner taxi forward onto the wide sea of concrete below him. He had already taken a brief look over the other passengers who would be travelling with him and had mentally decided that they were, without a single exception, a very dull and uninteresting lot. He had dismissed them from his mind, already having made it up, and resigning himself to the fact that he would have to content himself with watching the scenery below, what little he would see from above the clouds.

The tannoy system announced that the flight to Lisbon would be leaving in ten minutes and passengers should board the plane now waiting at bay three. Carradine had drunk two swift brandies before passing through the customs shed, but even this did not make him feel any easier in his mind. He never looked forward to being off the ground in one of these infernal contraptions as he preferred to call them; but there was no other way of travelling swiftly from one place to another and he was forced to forget his fear as best he could and put up with the inconvenience. It was a feeling of his which he could never explain. He could shoot a man in cold blood without turning a hair and could even apply one of the score or so methods of torture, all extremely painful, whenever it was necessary to extract information from an unwilling victim. Yet his stomach turned over whenever he was in the air.

He moved away from the window and joined a stream of passengers making their way along the white hall, down the stairs and out onto the tarmac where the jetliner stood waiting for them. The stewardess was standing at the bottom of the steps leading up into the belly of the plane, the list of passengers in her left hand. Carradine had lengthened his stride once they were outside the terminal buildings so that he was almost at the head of the small queue. If he had to travel by air, he preferred to get one of the seats as far back as possible. It was another foible of his, another little eccentricity he could not explain.

Lowering himself into the seat, he sat back with the carefully folded paper on his knee. There did not seem to be too many passengers on this flight and as he watched the others make their way forward, he hoped he would have this seat to himself. The faint whine of the jets sounded in his ears and seemed to vibrate through the very bones of his skull, setting up an unsympathetic ringing inside his head. Why anyone had ever claimed that these jets, with their terrible subsonics, were more comfortable to fly in than the older type of piston-engined aircraft, he had never been able to understand. Certainly they had the speed and were even more luxurious, but there were times when he felt as if his head were being split apart by that high-pitched whistle. It had occurred to him that, as certain animals were able to hear sounds pitched too high for human ears, so there might be some people who could pick up the sounds which were inaudible to the majority. Perhaps he was one of these unfortunate people, doomed to be bombarded by noises out of the range of sounds heard by others.

Now that the other passengers were seated, Carradine thrust his legs in front of him and leaned his head back. Very soon, the order to stop smoking and fasten their seat belts would go up above the distant cabin door and they would begin to taxi around the perimeter track to the end of the runway. He sucked in a deep gust of air, then glanced up sharply as a delicate whiff of perfume caught his nostrils and someone stopped beside him.

'Do you mind if I sit here?' The voice was warm, low and husky. Her hair was of a rich golden brown like ripening corn which only a few fortunate women possess, framing her face like a halo and falling in soft, natural waves to her shoulders. Her eyes were the most vivid blue that Carradine had ever seen. The faint trace of accent in her voice told him that she was not English.

'Not at all.' He looked at her seriously. A quick glance along the plane had confirmed that there were at least half a dozen empty seats further along which she could have taken. He smiled across at her as she sat down. Once again there was that faint whiff of perfume.

Carradine felt the girl's presence there very strongly. Her skin, he noticed, was slightly suntanned, pale golden brown, and her face bore little trace of make-up.

'I always find these flights so boring, don't you?' asked the girl.

Carradine jerked his gaze away from the scene outside, where the chocks were being pulled away from beneath the wheels. The whine of the jets rose swiftly to an almost ear-splitting crescendo.

'Sometimes.' Carradine took the cue. If there was an awareness that this gorgeous girl had chosen the seat next to him for some reason other than mere convenience, it remained tucked away in some tiny portion of his mind. Even so, he felt a vague, momentary disquiet. She smiled with the first faint hint of conspiracy.

'You are travelling to Portugal on holiday, or do you have business there, Mr . . . ?'

'My name is Carradine, Steve Carradine,' he said quietly. The plane was moving now, turning gently along the perimeter track, leaving the control buildings and customs behind in the sunlight.

'Mine is Solitaire duCann. My father is an exporter of wines. We have several vineyards in Portugal. Perhaps you have heard of the firm?'

Carradine shook his head slowly. 'I'm afraid not. This is my first visit to Portugal. My organisation deals in various metals and alloys. I'm hoping to be able to expand our export business now.'

'Then you must allow me to show you something of my country, Mr. Carradine. Most tourists tend to visit Spain rather than Portugal. They are missing a great deal by that.'

'I'm sure I would like that. I intend to stay at the Hotel Marrimos in Overo.' He glanced at her closely. 'Do you know it?'

'Certainly. You could not have chosen better.'

'I'm afraid I didn't choose it. My firm chose it for me. But I'll take your word for its excellence.'

Carradine sat back in his seat. They had already reached the end of the runway. The plane stood quite still for a long moment, the whining note of the jets changing abruptly. The pilot seemed to be running them at full power, yet keeping the brakes on, holding it there, throbbing and vibrating like a living creature, straining at the leash.

Then the brakes were suddenly released and the plane set off along the wide concrete strip of the runway, gathering speed and clawing at the heavens. The sun winked briefly in at the window next to Carradine's head, blinding him momentarily; and when he could see again, the trees and houses were doll-like under the plane and the banshee wail of the jets settled down to a faint, high-pitched whine, a background sound which Carradine forced out of his thoughts.

In less than ten minutes they were at eighteen thousand feet and heading into the wide air channel for the European flights.

Carradine unfastened his seatbelt. The plane rose steadily, high over the white sea of cloud. The sunlight, striking down on them, reflected back from all of that sheer whiteness, was dazzling, and after a few moments Carradine was forced to look away.

The girl had taken a book from the small bag at her feet and was browsing idly through the pages. Carradine took this opportunity to examine her a little more closely. In this sordid business in which he was engaged, he had long since learned never to take anything at its face value, even a highly beautiful woman who had, quite out of the blue, opened a conversation with him as if it were the most natural thing in the world; making an appointment to see him again, once they were in Portugal.

She was dressed in a simple style which told, however, of French influence. The skirt was neatly and closely pleated, flowing down from a slender waist. Her features were quite composed, as though she was totally unaware of his close scrutiny.

At length, she laid her book down on her lap. She gave him an amused glance. Sitting back in her seat, she closed her eyes for a moment, then said softly: 'I love travelling. One sees so many wonderful things, so many different places.'

Carradine gave her a look of inquiry. 'The wine business must really pay off.'

'It does,' she replied simply. 'But don't run away with the idea that I do nothing but enjoy myself. You could say that I'm an ambassador for the business. I leave all of the growing, the fermenting and bottling to my father and two brothers. I go out and bring in the orders from all over the world.'

Carradine smiled. 'There something to be said for that, I suppose. For myself, if I were a buyer of wines, I'd far sooner give a large order to you than to some fast-talking salesman. Perhaps you'll allow me to sample some of your wines. I pride myself on being something of a connoisseur.'

'But of course. I shall make a point of it.'

Through the window Carradine caught a brief glimpse of blue ocean spread out under them; then the fluffy cottonwood clouds swept in again and obscured it from sight. 'Has your family been in Portugal long?' he asked, turning.

He sensed her hesitation and saw the faint ghost of expression that flashed over her face. 'You're a very perceptive man,' she laughed. 'My name is not Portuguese. But my grandfather, who founded the business a little over sixty years ago, originally came from France. He liked Portugal, settled there, and started a business which has prospered over the years. Now we consider ourselves as Portuguese and not French, although there is a branch of the family still living only a few kilometres from Rouen.'

Lunch came, served to them on small metal trays. Carradine ate his slowly. There was still that vague queasy sensation in the pit of his stomach, but he gradually succeeded in ignoring it. While he ate, he gazed down at the green and brown land below them. The sea was never very far away and it was possible to make out the white strip of surf where it pounded on the rocks.

As he watched the ragged coastline moving slowly beneath them, he turned over in his mind the various possibilities that came to him concerning the activities of this enemy cell in Portugal. As yet, he did not know where they had their headquarters and was hoping that Corella would be able to give him a little information on this when they met. What could be their objective in Portugal? A forward base from which to spy on NATO naval exercises? A strong subversive group designed to deprive Britain of her oldest ally in the event of a shooting war?

There seemed to be so many possibilities, and yet not one of them seemed to fit the facts he had at his disposal. On the face of things, it didn't make sense. There were so many other countries where the enemy could concentrate men of the calibre of Varandashky. They would not waste his undoubted talents on something of little importance.

He went through in his mind what he had read in the two files which the Chief had given him to peruse. The facts that were known had proved to be extremely scanty.

VARANDASHKY: Substantive rank of Colonel. One-time member of the NKVD and has been known to act as an assassin under the control of the KGB. First came to the notice of the British Secret Service seven years before when operating in Turkey. His rise to power has been virtually meteoric, something uncommon in the Soviet Union, where every man is checked and double-checked for his loyalty to the party machine.

He is known to have been personally responsible for the deaths of three Secret Service agents and operated for a short period in America, where he is regarded as a most dangerous professional spy. He has twice succeeded in slipping through the fingers of the FBI just as the net was closing in on him and, on one occasion, a member of the FBI was arrested and tried on a charge of passing information to Varandashky which had enabled him to flee the country within hours of the FBI moving in on him.

No photographs are available of this man, but he is known to be well-built, around six feet tall, weight around two hundred and fifty pounds, well versed in the basic judo and karate holds. The fact that he had been awarded the Order of Lenin is sufficient testimony to his worth to the Russians.

Carradine closed the mental file in his mind and sat forward in his seat. A moment later the red light winked on above the door leading into the pilot's compartment. Obediently, he fastened the seatbelt and sat back, forcing his body to relax as the whine of the engines became deeper, more strident and the sound of air rushing past the plane became more and more audible. With an effort, he forced himself up to grip the sides of his seat as he glanced out of the window and saw the feathery clouds drift past them like smoke, then thin as they dropped through the cloud layer. The ground loomed up at them. Details clarified and became clearly spread out. The roads, houses, the traffic below, took on the aspect of toys seen from a height. Then they were skimming over the houses and roads; through the window he caught a fragmentary glimpse of the runways criss-crossing the airport as the plane circled slowly and lined up with the runway.

There was a faint bump as the undercarriage touched down and a blurring rush of detail as they skimmed along the ground. Carradine closed his mind to the thoughts of the past and thought of what might lie in store for him here. It seemed impossible that there could be danger for him in this country, but he remembered what the Chief had said about jumping to conclusions, particularly as they so often turned out to be the wrong ones. Danger always lurked where one least expected it, ready to jump out and overwhelm him before he had a chance to gear himself to meet it.

Five minutes later he climbed out of the plane and saw the white-walled airport buildings gleaming with a strange translucence in the sunlight. The warmth of the air touched a hand to his brow as he walked beside the girl across the tarmac towards the wire barrier. They went into the customs shed together.

Carradine's passport merely described him as a dealer in semi-precious metals. The official glanced at it briefly and looked up to compare the photograph with him.

'Are you here on business, sir?' he asked politely.

Carradine shrugged. 'Let's say business and — ' He glanced briefly at the girl beside him. ' — pleasure, whenever I can get any time away from my work.'

The official smiled knowingly, nodded, folded the passport and handed it back to him. 'I sincerely hope that you enjoy your stay in Portugal.'

'I'm quite sure I will.' Carradine slid the passport back into his breast pocket.

His luggage had been checked and was waiting for him at the end of the long counter. He picked it up and stood waiting for Solitaire. She joined him a few moments later.

'I always get through the customs here with the minimum of trouble,' she said. 'They know me by now. It has become almost a ritual.'

Carradine nodded and smiled a little. He wondered what the customs officials would have said had they decided to take him into the small room at the rear of the building and search him thoroughly, as they did with some of the people arriving here. The heavy Luger was strapped just beneath his left arm in a stiff leather holster which only just prevented the gun from being too obvious. Not to mention the various other articles of his trade which he was forced to carry on his person. No doubt they would have been both interested and surprised, too, if they had put his suitcase under the inspectroscope. It was highly unlikely that they would have marked his cases so quickly then.

Outside customs a tall, swarthy-faced man wearing a chauffeur's uniform stepped forward. He saluted as he came up to the girl and took her case.

'I have the car waiting, Miss duCann,' he said quietly. 'Your father asked me to take you directly to Oporto.'

The girl turned to Carradine. 'Can I offer you a lift, Mr. Carradine? Overo is on the way.'

Regretfully, Carradine declined. 'There should be someone here to meet me,' he said. 'But I'm quite sure that we shall meet again, very soon.'

'I know we shall.' She flashed him a quick smile, then turned and followed the chauffeur to the waiting car.

4

Don't Feed the Fishes

'I see you believe in travelling in expensive company, Mr. Carradine.'

Carradine whirled round. The girl had approached so quietly that he had not heard. He had been too intent on watching Solitaire duCann. Her hair was very black and shone in the sunlight, and although it was thick and heavy, it moved gently every time she moved her head. She did not keep touching it, or patting it to keep it in place. Her eyes were brown, set wide apart, and now they were watching him with an open candour that made him feel a trifle uncomfortable. There was even a touch of ironical calmness in them that tended to infuriate him a little, although he suppressed the feeling quickly. There was a white ribbon on the back of her hair, standing out in stark contrast to the raven blackness of it.

'How do you know my name?' he asked, forcing evenness into his tone. There was the faintly dying murmur of Solitaire's car in the street as it moved away, but this time he did not turn to follow it.

The girl held out her hand politely. 'I'm Veronique Corella. My father sent me to pick you up. He regrets that he could not come himself but some very important business came up which he had to attend to. He sends his apologies.'

'I'm sure he need not have bothered, when he sent such an admirable and attractive replacement.'

'You have a very pretty turn of compliments, Mr. Carradine,' the girl said softly.

'Won't you call me Steve?' He smiled. 'After all, we shall be seeing quite a lot of each other while I'm in Portugal.'

She arched her brows delicately. 'I understand that you came here to see my father.' The irony had crept into her voice once more. Turning, she led the way down the steps towards a racing car drawn up at the side of the road.

Carradine eyed it in faint surprise. The girl slipped in behind the wheel and motioned to the boot. 'You can put your luggage in there. I think it will hold it all.'

'Thanks.' Carefully, Carradine stowed his cases in the very spacious boot. To his expert eyes, it seemed obvious that the car had been modified a little from its original design. He doubted if the man who had designed it would recognise it now, although the alterations which had been carried out on it had been done by an expert and would pass all but the closest examination. He began to wonder what modifications had been made to the engine under the long, sleek bonnet.

The girl glanced sideways at him as he opened the door and got in. She raced the engine for a moment, her foot moving slowly on the accelerator pedal, then threw in the clutch, took off the brake and moved away from the kerb and into the stream of traffic. Carradine felt vaguely worried as he sat in silence beside her. The Chief had told him nothing of Corella having a daughter, nor that he would meet up with her like this. He wondered if she knew the kind of business he had to discuss with her father; whether she was in the other's confidence. This put him in a dilemma. He would have liked to have talked with her about the position here if possible, get a little knowledge of the situation, but that was out of the question until he knew just where she fitted into the picture. He decided to play it safe and talk only of general things.

Before he could say anything, however, she said quietly: 'Where did you meet your charming companion? On the plane? Or in London?'

He glanced at her in momentary surprise. There was an odd little edge to her voice which he couldn't quite fathom. 'You mean Solitaire duCann?'

'That's right. She isn't exactly the sort of companion I would have expected you to have teamed up with, even on the short flight from London.'

'What do you know of her then?' His tone was quite innocent.

'Nothing much that I could prove. Her father owns a large wine-making and marketing concern in northern Portugal.'

'And is there anything wrong in that?'

'Perhaps.' She seemed intent on being evasive. 'My father knows the details more precisely than I do. We have had some contact with them before. That is why I kept in the background until she had gone.'

'I see.'

She shook her head, taking him literally at his word. 'Somehow I don't think you do. They came from France about sixty years ago and settled here in Portugal.'

'I know. She told me that.'

Veronique pursed her lips and pressed her foot down a little more on the accelerator. The needle on the speedometer crept swiftly up to the eighty mark, the air streaming past their heads now, a faint whistle in Carradine's ears. Fortunately, now that they had left Lisbon behind, there seemed to be little traffic on the road. He had the feeling that the girl was doing this deliberately, her face glowing a little, lips parted now as she swung the little car around a slow-moving vehicle, regaining her lane once more.

'I've no doubt that she told you a great many things, but how many of them are anywhere near the truth is another matter entirely. She's very beautiful, perhaps.' Veronique said this as if she was speaking about a piece of porcelain or an animal in some cage in the zoo. 'But she can also be very dangerous.'

'To men or women?' Carradine asked, glancing obliquely at her from the side of his vision.

'To both I'm afraid,' replied the other, quite unperturbed by his remark. 'If you continue to see her, I'm certain you will eventually find that out to your cost.' She paused and concentrated on her driving for a long moment, staring directly ahead of her in taut silence. This was a bad start, Carradine thought. The girl had now decided that he was being offhand with her and he wondered what he might do to retrieve the situation. He had already found that she was not too amenable to flattery.

'I'm sorry you don't agree with my taste. In my own defence, I must point out that the meeting was none of my choosing. She simply sat down next to me on the plane and started a conversation.'

The girl's face assumed a serious look. 'Maybe she saw your name on the passenger list. Yes, that must be the explanation.'

'I'm afraid I don't understand. Even if she did, why should she — ?'

'Because we have every reason to believe that she may be an agent for the Reds.' She chuckled a little. 'Does that really surprise you? Or is your male ego such that you believe every woman will inevitably throw herself at your feet?'

Carradine felt suitably chastened by her remark. He sat up a little straighter in his seat. 'Not really.' He smiled faintly. 'What makes you think that she may be working for the other side?'

'There is a suspicion — nothing more you understand — that they are associated with an international smuggling ring which is often merely another front for a Red organisation.' Her smile became tight. 'As one of the country's biggest wine exporters, they naturally have a far greater licence to operate without stricter government supervision than most other concerns in Portugal. Of course, the police authorities have been unable to prove anything directly against them, otherwise they would have been forced to take action. But there was an unpleasant episode just over a year ago.'

Carradine raised his brows expressively and waited for her to go on. It was beginning to appear that Solitaire duCann was something of a tiger in the guise of a beautiful woman.

'Nobody knows the real details. The entire thing was hushed up by the police for some reason. The facts are that two bodies were washed ashore near Overo. One of them was subsequently identified as a man who worked for François duCann. The other was never identified. All that was known was that he had a strange birthmark on his left shoulder. 'It was in the shape of a cross. Both bodies were almost unrecognisable. They had been in the water for only two or three days, but — '

'You're suggesting that they were perhaps deliberately mutilated before they were dropped into the water, just in case they were ever washed up on shore and someone started inquiries?'

'Perhaps. My father had his own suspicions. He had some influence with the local chief of police in Overo and he was given permission to see the bodies before they were taken away. He said that — ' She hesitated for a moment, then gave a long blast on the horn as the car ahead of them tried to pull out into the lane. ' — in his opinion, the sharks had got to them.'

'Sharks?' Carradine looked puzzled. 'Surely there are very few sharks off these coasts. Even those you do find are basking sharks. That species very rarely attacks human beings.'

'That is what my father said. But he also believes that there is something — some chemical perhaps — which can be smeared on a man's body and not washed off too easily by the sea water, something that will attract sharks and drive them wild.'

Carradine turned that over in his mind. The idea was distinctly plausible. But why would anyone go to all that trouble just to dispose of two men? The sea water could not be guaranteed to wash all traces of such a chemical from the bodies and once traces of it were discovered, the fact that the men's deaths were not accidental would be clear. He forced a sudden, bitter smile. They were not in England now. The methods used by the police in this country were not as refined as those employed by the pathologists at New Scotland Yard, and even these scientists might be forgiven for overlooking such a remote possibility. Nevertheless, there was still a nagging little germ of suspicion in his mind. When they reached Overo he would get in touch with liaison in London and have them check on the possible identity of a man having a birthmark on his left shoulder in the shape of a cross. It was a long shot and one fired in the dark, but he had the feeling that in this particular case he was going to need every scrap of information he could get. There seemed to be so many new angles popping up at every turn.

'Do you know if the case on those two men has been closed?' he asked, sitting back and closing his eyes lazily, feeling the languorous touch of the sun on his upturned face. The breeze stirred his hair and he judged, without looking at the speedometer, that there were doing between ninety and a hundred. The road was not ideal for such fast driving, but the girl seemed well able to control the car. In fact, he thought, she was one hell of a good driver — and she knew it.

'Knowing the way the police act in this country, particularly out here on the coast, I would think it highly probable that they have. They always seem particularly averse to keeping cases on their files any longer than they can help. It offends tidy minds leaving unsolved cases to clutter up the place. Besides, François duCann is a very important man. A word from him in all of the right places and no further action is taken.'

'In might therefore be worthwhile to have a little talk with him. You make him sound a very interesting character.'

'More interesting than Solitaire?' queried the girl archly. She glanced in the driving mirror and stiffened abruptly.

'Something wrong?' Carradine asked sharply.

'I'm not sure. That car back there has been following us the last three or four kilometres. They may be nothing, but on the other hand, if you were recognised at the airport and they knew your real business here . . . ' She left the rest of the sentence unsaid.

Carradine turned on his feet. Quite suddenly he was acutely aware of the welcome feel of the Luger nestling against the side of his chest. The car was perhaps half a kilometre away, neither gaining on them nor falling back. It was as if there was an invisible rod between them, holding them rigidly apart so that one was forced to faithfully imitate the movements of the other.

'It could be just a coincidence,' he said harshly, 'but I don't like it. You don't recognise the car, do you, Veronique?'

'One of those high-powered German cars,' she replied without hesitation. 'Better watch out now. I'll open her up. See if we can throw them off at all.' The tiny sports car leapt forward as if shot from the barrel of a gun. They tore around a wide curve with the sun a glittering blue on the sea on their left. Now they were doing a hundred and ten, a hundred and twenty. For a moment, the other car drifted gently away from them as their speed increased. Then it was all too evident that it was beginning to catch up on them again, narrowing the intervening distance.

'No doubt at all about it now,' Carradine muttered thinly. 'They're closing the gap, slowly but surely.' Reaching inside his jacket, he pulled out the heavy Luger, thumbing off the safety catch. He had made up his mind. He had no other alternative. There was no other traffic on the coast road and it was obvious that the men in that car behind knew their business. They must have been waiting for him at the airport and had followed the sports car, which would have stood out in a crowd, at a very discreet distance, mingling with the traffic until they were out here where they could run the sports car over the side of the cliff, down into the sea where they would probably feed the fishes as those other two poor devils had. He no longer doubted that either duCann or Varandashky was behind this, pulling the strings from somewhere in the shadows.

Coincidence piled on coincidence soon built an edifice that spelled a definite plan of campaign being enacted against them.

'What are you going to do?' asked the girl. Her voice was a shout to make herself heard above the whine of the wind rushing past their ears and the roar of the tyres on the rough surface of the road.

'I'm going to try to get in the first shot,' he called back. 'Just keep your head down as much as you can. They'll almost certainly start shooting back.'

'All right, Steve. But be careful. I'll try to hold the car as steady as I can.'

'Just you concentrate on keeping us on the road.' He caught a brief, blurred glimpse of the rugged jumble of rocks that lay piled high at the foot of the cliff down to their left as they swerved around a sharply angled bend. For a second he felt sure she had got into an uncontrollable skid. There was the high-pitched, piercing screech of the tyres at the road surface. Then they were round, temporarily out of sight of their pursuers.

Squirming around in his seat, Carradine rested the heavy gun on the smooth metalwork of the car. It was not the ideal perch for it, but the best there was in the circumstances. His finger was hard on the trigger, taking up the slack. Leaning forward a little, he waited, legs braced against the floor of the car, steadying himself against the swaying, jolting motion. Now that they had discovered how impossible it was to shake off the other car by sheer speed, Veronique had slowed to eighty and was trying to hold the car steady at that. Even so, it was not going to be easy getting in a killing shot under such conditions.

Tension built up in the hot, wind-rushing afternoon. They were now on a comparatively straight stretch of the road. Seconds later the black saloon car swept into view around the corner. Carradine caught a glimpse of a deathly white face crouching over the steering wheel, and of another figure seated beside the driver. The second man was now winding down the window at his side. He leaned out of it almost casually, as if savouring the cool air that swept about him. What looked suspiciously like a Schmeisser was cradled in his hands, the barrel pointed along the length of the front wing of the car. Squinting quickly, Carradine squeezed the trigger. The Luger jerked viciously in his hand, kicking back against his wrists. He saw the neat hole appear as if by magic in the windscreen of the other car, with a tiny circular pattern of cracked glass around it like a halo.

Then the Schmeisser chatted briefly. Carradine saw the vivid orange flashes from the end of the barrel, heard the low hum of the slugs cutting through the air over his head as he crouched down. A bullet hit the side of the car and ricocheted off, tearing a burning gash along his arm. It felt as if a white-hot poker had been suddenly laid against his flesh.

Sucking in a sharp gust of air, he aimed and fired again, missing completely as the girl swerved the car at the same moment. Carradine bit down on the curse that rose unbidden to his lips, then saw why the girl had done it. She must have spotted the danger in the driving mirror, taking the only course she could. The stream of bullets from the Schmeisser whistled evilly over his head, missing him by scant inches. Seconds later, she levelled off the car once more, the tyres screeching in protest.

Very soon they would hit another shaking, twisting section of the road and there would be very little chance of him aiming accurately then. His palms were slippery with sweat and it trickled from his forehead into the hair of his eyebrows and down into his eyes, half-blinding him. He thought of the girl sitting beside him and knew that if he failed now she would share the same fate as himself. The thought steadied the swirling turmoil in his mind and forced the strength back into his body. They weren't dead yet, not by a long way. Damn it, he would finish these men before they had the chance to kill the girl and himself! He tensed his muscles, focused his mind more sharply, and blinked the sweat out of his eyes.

The gunman had withdrawn the

Schmeisser and was slipping a fresh magazine into the weapon. Carradine got off one shot that struck the side of the car. Then the man was leaning out of the window again. Carradine could see the leering features beneath the soft felt hat drawn well down over the eyes, and the tight gash of the mouth, lips drawn back to reveal the teeth. He fired again, getting off a snap shot as the other began to line up the gun on him. The man jerked his body stiffly and threw back his head as if he had been struck by an uppercut on the chin. The look on his face changed abruptly. He seemed to have grown a third eye in the centre of his forehead; a blank, open eye that oozed tears of blood. Then the gun fell from his nerveless fingers, was caught up by the swiftly spinning wheels and hurled back and away into the cloud of white dust that lifted behind the speeding car. The driver leaned sideways, caught at the plunging arm and pulled the other inside, where the body slumped against the seat.

That was one menace removed effectively, Carradine thought grimly, but the real danger still remained. Slowly, the gap between the two cars was narrowing as the other piled on the pressure, his foot clearly hard down on the accelerator pedal. The girl was forced to brake hard as they hit an uneven patch of road where a recent landslide had sent rock and rubble hurtling down the side of the cliff to their right, strewing the road with boulders. Most of the rock had been removed but there were still some good-sized boulders lying around. The car behind was coming up far too fast to see them in time, and the driver had probably missed the warning sign by the side of the road when he had been busy pulling in his companion's dead body. Now he had to jam on his brakes hard, gripping the wheel furiously as the car threatened to skid out of control. The wheels slammed into a couple of rocks, which threatened to hurl the car over the edge. By a miracle the other managed to keep the saloon on the road, but it had been a near thing.

'Think you can manage to hold off?' Carradine yelled in the girl's ear. He slipped back into the seat beside her.

'I'm not so sure. I'll try my best. He must have supercharged that engine to be able to get that kind of speed out of it.' There was a noticeable look of excitement on her face. A few minutes later she said tightly: 'There is one chance if you're prepared to take it. A very slender one, I'm afraid, and it will depend on split-second timing on our part.'

'Whatever it is, we'll have to try it. That killer behind us means to force us off the road as soon as he gets the chance.'

'Then listen carefully,' said Veronique urgently. 'There's a very narrow bridge less than a kilometre from here. No place to pass on either side of it, especially for a big car like that. I'm going to try to stop the car in the middle of the road on top of the bridge and take a chance on there being no traffic coming the other way. We have to get out and under the bridge before he gets there. You understand?'

Carradine nodded tautly. 'Will he have time to pull up before he hits the car?'

Veronique shook her head grimly. 'There won't be a chance for him if we can pull it off,' she said dispassionately. 'Now hold on and be ready when I give the word.'

What a cold-blooded little minx she was, mused Carradine. Here she was, casually planning to murder the driver of the car behind them, without a thought for her own personal safety. Carradine tensed himself and focused all of his senses on what lay ahead. It was a gamble, but the only chance they had. The wind, screaming around them now as they plunged into a vicious hairpin descent, brought tears streaming from his eyes. He thrust the Luger back into the stiff leather holster beneath his left arm. Somehow he had the feeling it would not be needed if the girl's plan worked at all. The pursuing car was temporarily lost to sight behind the huge outcrop of rock. They had managed to pull back a little of the distance on the other when he had been forced to swerve to control the big, heavy saloon as he had hit the rocky patch on the road.

'There it is, Steve,' called Veronique.

Turning back, Carradine glanced through

the low windscreen. The road twisted once, still downgrade, and narrowed swiftly as it crossed the humpback bridge. There were high, solid stone walls on either side of the bridge and a stream poured down the side of the cliff and under the bridge, then plummeted for another fifty feet or so to the rock-strewn beach directly below.

The girl put her foot hard on the brakes. Their speed dropped sickeningly. Carradine braced himself as the treacherous deceleration forced his body forward out of the low seat. No time to look round now and see if the saloon was yet in sight.

How Veronique managed it he was not sure, but less than ten seconds later she had brought the car to a screeching but controlled halt right on top of the bridge in the middle of the narrow stretch of road, completely blocking it.

'Now!' cried the girl. He had a quick impression of her struggling to her feet and clambering over the top of the car door — there was no room whatever in which to open it properly — and on top of the wide stone parapet. Within seconds he was beside her, one arm around her slender waist. Together they dropped onto the large flat-topped slab of rock beside the swift-running stream.

For a moment they hung poised; then they were under the arch of the bridge itself, crouched against the moist slabs of curved stone, feeling the heavy drops of icy cold water that dripped continually onto the tops of their heads from the ceiling of the bridge less than six inches above them. Scarcely were they there than the shrill bleat of rubber tearing at the road reached their ears, oddly muffled by the stone, but quite unmistakable.

Now what? thought Carradine. His mind felt strangely empty and hollow. The rending, tearing crash as a ton or more of metal ploughed into the back of the sports car perched somewhere above their heads, standing so innocently on top of the bridge? Or had the other seen the warning blink of red from their lights and been able to brake in time to avoid a collision? If he had, the odds were that he would come hunting for them with the Schmeisser.

The screech of protesting rubber stopped quite suddenly, as abruptly as if the car had been snatched up off the road by some gigantic hand. Carradine felt his muscles coil. The girl clutched tightly at him, her slim fingers biting into the flesh of his injured arm, making him gasp with the agony of it. She linked her arm through his. Her eyes were very wide, her red lips parted, her breathing faster and more shallow than usual. She seemed to be in the grip of emotions he could not begin to understand. He felt sure it was not fear there in her mind.

He looked at her quietly. 'He must have somehow been able to stop in time,' he said harshly. 'It's the only explanation.' He tugged the Luger from its holster and thumbed off the catch. 'Now we shall have to go out and look for him; kill him before he kills us.'

The crash sounded oddly muffled, far more so than could be explained by the dulling columns of stone on all sides of them, and it had not come from directly above them as they had been expecting.

'What on earth happened?' asked the

girl breathlessly. They scrambled to their feet and splashed through the few inches of water at the very edge of the stream to the opening. Carradine reached the large flat rock and pulled himself up on it. There was dead silence all about them — not a sound. Or was there? A faint crackling noise that he could not quite place. Clearly it was not what he had expected to hear. Lifting his head, he squinted into the strong sunlight, back along the stretch of road where it wound up to the top of the cliff. The tyre marks left by the sports car were clearly visible. He looked for some sign of the skid marks left by the saloon. For a moment he could see nothing. Puzzled, he stepped forward and clambered up onto the road. Then he switched his gaze abruptly as the realisation of what must have happened came to him in a flash. The black skid marks stopped some twenty yards away, just at the point where they were beginning to curve away off the road.

He knew now what had happened in those few brief moments after the driver had seen the obstruction which faced him. He had seen the parked car much too late to be able to stop. Instinctive reflexes had taken over control of his body. He had swerved sharply to the left, hoping perhaps to guide the car around the rearing parapet of the bridge. Either he had hauled much too hard on the wheel, or he had realised at the last moment the impossibility of getting a car through that narrow gap. Whatever had gone on in his fear-crazed mind, crouching over the wheel with the dead body of his companion lolling in the seat beside him, he had gone over the edge of the cliff, hurtling out into empty space, plummeting down through those fifty feet to oblivion. Now the saloon lay in a heap of mangled metal, barely recognisable for what it was, scattered on the sharp-toothed rocks down below, a faint red lick of flame coming from it.

Veronique came forward and stood beside him, staring down. She had the back of her hand pressed tightly against her mouth.

'Is he dead, do you think?' she asked in a hushed whisper.

'I would think so.' Carradine's tone was cold, hard and utterly emotionless. He had known too many men like this, ruthless and cruel men who carried out the murderous orders of the various big international organisations. 'He probably never knew what hit him. Once he went over the edge there would be just a split second before he hit the bottom and it was all over.'

'Do you think we ought to go down there and make absolutely certain before we leave?'

'What would be the use of that? After all, we . . . ' He broke off sharply, instinctively putting up an arm over his face as the boiling burst of flame, accompanied by an explosion, soared up at them as the petrol tank went up. A gout of red-tongued flame completely engulfed the car in seconds. Sickened a little in spite of the tight grip he had on himself, Carradine backed away from the edge of the cliff, drawing the girl with him onto the road.

'Let's get out of here,' he said harshly. 'Any time now this whole area will be swarming with police, and I don't feel like having to answer any of their inane questions right now.'

Unresisting, the girl got back into the car. She sat for a long moment behind the wheel, then glanced down at his arm. A look of concern flashed over her features. 'You've been hurt,' she said sharply.

'It's nothing. Just a flesh wound. That gunman with the Schmeisser was a little more accurate than he knew.'

She stared up at him for a moment, then switched on the ignition. The powerful engine roared into ecstatic life. Three minutes later they had driven around a further bend in the road, and the thick column of oily black smoke was lost from sight behind them.

* * *

'It seems rather a pity you were forced to deal so drastically — and permanently — with these two men,' said Corella softly. He sipped his brandy slowly as if intent on savouring every single mouthful before swallowing it. 'We could almost certainly have wrung something of importance from them.'

'Only if they had been sufficiently co-operative as to talk,' Carradine replied. 'Whoever is at the back of these hired killers holds them with a steel chain which they find impossible to break.'

Corella smiled. 'There are ways of making men talk, even men such as these. They are not nice ways, nor for the squeamish, but this is a war we are fighting in which there are no rules whatsoever.' His gaze rested on Carradine. 'Now that they know you are here in Portugal we must watch every single move we make. I had hoped that they would not notice your arrival.' He shrugged eloquently. 'That hope is irretrievably gone, so we must be like the cat with eight lives already used up, no?' He grinned broadly and this time there was mirth and warmth on his face. He finished the brandy and placed the empty glass on the table in front of him, his huge, hairy paw still fastened almost incongruously around the delicately fashioned stem of the brandy glass.

Carradine nodded. He felt himself warming to the other. There were few men he felt like this about at first sight. He felt there was a tremendous air of vitality about Corella. He exuded confidence. The kind of man, Carradine decided, who faced every problem, every task — short of the completely impossible — with a determined will to win. It was the sort of positive outlook so necessary in a man in his position.

'Veronique was telling me of the two bodies which were washed ashore near here about a year ago.' Carradine sat back in the comfortable chair. 'Is it possible for me to get a message through to liaison in London fairly soon?'

Corella knit his brows together for a moment. 'That can be arranged,' he said, puzzled. 'It will take an hour to set up the connections. You have something on your mind?'

'It may be nothing at all. That man who was found was never identified, but he had a curious birthmark on his left shoulder. It may be that they will be able to identify him for us.'

'Why should they know this man?'

'We have several agents working in this area. Some have disappeared without trace over the past few years.' Carradine's tone was flat, soft.

'Ah, my friend, now I understand.' The tension had gone out of the other's voice. 'You think that this man may have been one of your agents?' He pursed his lips and nodded. 'Yes, it is quite possible. I must confess that the idea had not occurred to me. That is a mistake.' He tapped a broad finger against the side of his nose. 'I can usually tell when there is something wrong. I felt it that time when I learned of those two men. And when one of them was a man working for duCann, then I tried to — How do you say it? — put two and two together. But I got no further. I tried to get the police to investigate a little further, but they refused.

'François duCann maintained that this man of his had taken a friend out with him to do some fishing out in the bay, in spite of the warnings he had been given that the weather was worsening. And there were also dangerous rocks just beneath the surface which could tear the bottom out of a boat as if it were made of paper. Naturally, the police believed his story. There was no reason for them not to do so. They were quite satisfied, and the two bodies were taken away and buried. Now the affair has been forgotten, except perhaps by men such as you and me, and maybe François duCann.'

Carradine made no comment. There was a knock on the door and Veronique came in with the coffee. She set the silver tray down on the table, glancing knowingly from one man to the other.

'What have you two been hatching together while I have been away?' she asked. 'Something to do with duCann?'

'Perhaps.' Corella barked out a harsh laugh. 'Sometimes I think that I have a man here instead of a woman, the way she handles my fears.'

Carradine smiled, keeping his eyes fixed on Veronique as he said: 'There are some of us who prefer her as she is. I must confess I would count it as a great loss if that were true.'

He was rewarded by the faint pink blush that rose unbidden to the girl's face. She said quietly: 'You have, as I said before, a very pretty turn of compliments. But one which may someday get you into big trouble.'

'I'll promise to keep my eyes open for it.'

'Only a fool would make a promise like that,' she said, but her smile robbed the words of any malice. 'I hope you will keep it though. I would hate to see you brought out of the water like those other two, or burnt to a cinder in some smashed car piled up on the rocks.'

5

A Shaft of Moonlight

There was more coffee brought that evening as the two men took each piece of evidence and information they possessed, looked at it, discussed it, and then dissected it, putting aside that which could be discarded and keeping that which seemed to have some bearing, however indirectly, on Carradine's assignment.

Finally, Corella closed the bulky file with a smack. 'There you have it. All that I know to be fact. I have my own suspicions, but to tell those may lead you along the wrong path entirely. There is something going on in the Red camp inside Portugal. I feel, indeed I know, most of it is concentrated around here, around Overo. There have been various comings and goings.

'Now this attack on you has brought

things to a head. There is something here which you should get away from, but I know that nothing I can say or do will make you take the next plane out of Lisbon back to London. I have the feeling that somewhere, maybe very close by, a plan is being laid against you. That was a very crude attempt to kill you that they made this afternoon. The next time they try — and believe me there will be a next time — it will be something far more refined and subtle. They will now know the kind of opponent they face. How much they know of you and your reasons for being here, that I do not know. But I think it is more than sufficient for them to know that you represent a grave danger to them and that it is imperative for them to remove you permanently as soon as they possibly can.'

Carradine drained his coffee and sat back. Through the open window that looked out over the wide sweep of the bay, the sunset was a brilliant mixture of golds and reds and greens, all blending overhead into a deep blue-purple that had to be seen to be believed. The sea was calm, with only the faint splash of the surf as it rolled in a diagonal line of white onto the sand. Outside, it was so utterly peaceful and calm that it seemed impossible for there to be trouble and danger here, bubbling away like some hellish witch's brew just beneath the surface.

'That island out there in the bay,' he said, pointing. 'Does anyone live there?'

Corella glanced in the direction of his pointing finger and shook his head. 'I have heard on no occasion of anyone living there. It used to be a wild bird sanctuary, although whether anyone ever goes there now is doubtful. A few of the fisher folk, perhaps, but that is all. Why are you interested in it? Merely because of its charm?'

'I was still thinking about those dead men washed up on the shore. It seems to me that the incoming tide is just in the right direction to sweep them in from there. It might even be worth a visit.'

'Wasn't there some talk that someone had tried to purchase that island, Father?' said the girl softly. She stood by the side of the window, looking out over the scene below. 'I seem to recall that some foreigner had offered to buy it.'

'As far as I'm aware, nothing came of it. The government were not anxious to sell. You are quite right; there was someone anxious to buy it. They even went out there on several occasions to look over the place. A desolate piece of land, good for nothing but to keep a few million birds happy.'

'And perhaps a few of our non-feathered friends also,' said Carradine grimly. 'I'm more certain than ever that it will be worth a visit, a very discreet one of course.'

'And how do you propose to do that?' asked Corella furiously. 'If there does happen to be anyone there, they could see you long before you reached the island.'

'Not if I was to get there underwater,' Carradine said easily.

'Skin-diving,' said Veronique. 'How exciting.'

'And dangerous,' Carradine put in. 'I wasn't asking for company.'

She pouted at him. 'Nevertheless, I

shall insist on coming with you. Just in case you get into the same kind of trouble you did this afternoon. You can't say I panicked then, or lost my head.'

'No, but that was a situation we were forced into. I'm going into this one with my eyes open.'

'And when are you going to do this?'

'Tomorrow,' Carradine said decisively. He looked across to the girl. 'If you wish to help you can row me out to the middle of the bay and wait to pick me up again.'

'I call that grossly unfair,' she countered, 'but if it is the condition, then I agree.'

'And now, my friend,' said Corella, scraping back his chair and getting to his feet. 'Are you sure that you will not accept my invitation to remain here for the night? We are always glad to have guests with us and I assure you that — '

'Nothing would have given me greater pleasure than to accept your kind offer. But I did make a reservation at the Hotel Marrimos. It may look suspicious if I don't take it, and there is just a chance that these people haven't connected me with you. It would be best if we could leave it that way. The less they know about you, the better. I'm sure the Chief would prefer you to remain as anonymous as possible.'

'Perhaps you are right. But be careful, my friend. Even in such a place as the Hotel Marrimoss there can be danger when one least expects it. You understand?'

'Perfectly. I doubt if they will try again so soon after their fiasco this afternoon, but if they do I shall sleep with one eye open and one hand on this.' He brought out the Luger, holding it tightly in his right hand.

'An excellent weapon,' said Corella, nodding. 'I find that it is difficult to get off shots rapidly with such a gun, but by the time the first has been fired somebody is dead.'

Veronique went with him to the door. There was a veiled look of concern on her face. She said softly: 'Be very careful, Steve. There are many people here in Portugal, possibly in Overo, who want you dead.'

'I'll be careful,' he said. He looked down

at the girl's profile in the dim light; at the red lips, parted a little to reveal the white, even teeth; the black hair that shone smoothly in the dimness, falling in long, natural waves onto her neck and shoulders. Acting on impulse, he leaned forward and kissed her softly on the lips. For a moment she strained away from him. Then, without warning or explanation, her arms went tightly around him and she responded to his kiss almost fiercely.

When she drew back, there was a strange look in her eyes which he had not seen before.

'Now listen, Veronique,' he said firmly, holding her by the shoulders. He fixed his gaze on her hair, shining in the light from the doorway. 'I suppose you know almost as much about these people we're fighting as I do. You know that they play for keeps. I don't want you to go with me tomorrow out to that island. Just in case there is trouble.'

He had meant to say that whenever one was in this sort of business a woman like Veronique was your second body. She made another target for a gunman's bullet; made it impossible for you to concentrate with a singleness of purpose and design on the job in hand. But he saw a shadow across her eyes. It was not one of fear; far from it. Her next words confirmed this.

'I'm not afraid of these men. With my father, I've been fighting them for almost as long as I can remember. I know it was a shock to me when I first learned what he really did. He tried to keep it from me at the beginning, both because he did not want me to get mixed up in it, and because it was his job to work in secret. But one day I found out — I discovered the radio transmitter he keeps hidden in the base of the house; I found out why he had to go there at a certain time every day to receive a call from London. Then there was nothing he could do but to tell me everything.'

'And you have been helping him ever since,' said Carradine gently. He still held her, feeling the warm flesh under his fingers. He wondered if the Chief knew of this. Certainly the other had not mentioned a word about the girl to him, and he would have thought that if he knew of her existence and her work in this matter he would have done so. Perhaps he ought to have a word with the other about it when he got back to London — *if* he got back.

'You could call it patriotism, I suppose,' the girl was saying. 'But somehow I've never looked at it that way. It was just something which seemed to me to be the natural thing to do.'

'And you do it extremely well, Veronique,' he said. 'But there is no sense in putting yourself in danger deliberately. These people will stop at nothing to gain their ends.'

'But you will let me take you out there?' There was a note almost of pleading in her voice. 'If you do get into trouble, perhaps I could help. I can use a gun and I'm not afraid to do so.'

'All right.' He patted her on the arm. 'I'll come around at ten o'clock and will take a look at that bird sanctuary in the bay. Maybe there is nothing there after all, but it's as well to be sure.'

* * *

The elevator door slid aside with a faint whisper of well-oiled metal on metal. Carradine stepped out into the short corridor, following the porter. The other unlocked his room, handed the key to him, went inside and placed the heavy suitcase on the wooden stand before bowing himself out and closing the door softly behind him. Turning the key in the lock, Carradine moved into the middle of the room. He had not expected such luxury in the Hotel Marrimos. In the big hotels in Lisbon perhaps, but not here. Evidently Portugal was striving to make itself more of a tourist attraction with each passing year, hoping to lure some of the richer people away from Spain, her next-door neighbour.

Moonlight was beginning to filter through the curtains across a wide balcony window and a cool breeze blew in off the sea. Taking off his jacket and shirt, he went into the bathroom, brushed his teeth and gargled with mouthwash before switching off the pink-shaded light. He did not put on the light in the bedroom, but padded over to the window and twitched the curtains aside, holding them open with his hands. The moon was still low on the horizon, touching the outline of the sea, dividing it off from the long, curved stretch of the smooth, sandy beach. A few palms waved long, fronded leaves languidly in the soft night air.

A truly luxurious setting, he thought. Far better than the hot, sultry days he had experienced in London. If only there wasn't duCann and Varandashky to worry about, everything would be ideal. He rubbed his fingers over the short stubble on his chin. Why did his mind persist in linking these two together like this? He had absolutely no proof whatsoever that duCann was working with Varandashky. Certainly the wine exporter was mixed up in something, and it might well be something that Corella would have to keep an eye on, but that was his affair and nothing to do with him. He was after the Russian, his purpose to find out what was going on here in Portugal. The fact that he was stirring up a hornet's nest was obvious after what had happened on his first day in the country.

Going over to the chair where he had draped his jacket, he checked the Luger, slipping the slender bullets into the spring-loaded magazine and thrusting it back with a sharp click into the butt of the weapon. This was a gun he was used to, the weapon which had saved his life on countless occasions in the past. Now it was an inseparable part of him.

He laid it on the small table beside the bed where it gleamed bluely in the shaft of moonlight. The faint murmur of the surf in the distance as it crashed endlessly on the sand had a hypnotic quality, reminding him just how tired he was.

Slipping the gun under the pillow, he undressed and crawled into the bed. There was no sound outside apart from the surf and the occasional drone of a car somewhere in the town. The night breeze, sighing in through the window, was wonderfully cool on his face.

He felt uncommonly sleepy. Lying there, gazing at the moonlight on the floor, he tried to think things out again, but the drowsiness in his brain refused to let him. His thoughts kept slipping off at a tangent, becoming blurred and making little sense. Sleep came to him in great, enervating waves, sweeping over him in tune to the muted murmur of the sea.

He woke once as some faint sound outside stirred a responsive chord in his mind, in that part of the brain which did not sleep. The luminous hands on the wristwatch on the bedside table said eleven-fifteen. The place was very still and the sound that he had heard was not repeated. For a moment he debated within himself whether to get up and check on it, then decided it had been nothing, rolled over onto his side and went back to sleep.

The second time Carradine awakened he had been sleeping soundly, and it had not been a nightmare which had woken him. The hotel was deathly still; outside, the deep purple night of summer in Portugal was hung with stars and the brilliant face of the moon. He lay quite still beneath the blankets, staring intently into the darkness.

The window of the room was not

closed, the curtains blowing a little in the wind, and a beam of moonlight lay across the floor of his room, reaching now almost to the bed in which he lay. Intently, he watched that yellow beam of light. It was getting wider very slowly, scarcely perceptibly.

There was no sound, although the window was half-open now; and a moment later he saw the barrel of the gun coming through, the moonlight glinting bluely off the smooth metal. Gradually, the gun tilted until it was pointing directly at his bed and he could see the finger on the trigger; could see the shadow of the assassin blotting out the patch of moonlight on the floor.

Very slowly, making no sound, Carradine eased his hand under the pillow near his head. His fingers touched metal and a moment later closed around the butt of the gun. He slipped it gently towards him, not once taking his eyes off the dark shape showing in the window. Cautiously he moved his legs, an inch at a time. His mind kept screaming frantically at him to hurry; that at any moment that finger might tighten the pressure on the trigger and send a bullet homing into his heart, but he ignored the voice of panic. Instead he slid his body along beneath the smooth sheet until his legs were touching the floor on the far side of the bed. He held his breath, acutely aware of the thumping of his heart against his ribs and the tiny trickle of sweat that had formed on his forehead, now oozing irritatingly down the side of his nose. He forced himself to ignore everything but the danger which now confronted him.

The dark, ill-defined figure eased further into the room. There was a faint creak of wood as the window was pushed further open and the figure stiffened in sudden reflex, pausing as if listening for any movement Carradine might make. Then it began to move through again, slipping into the room. Now Carradine could make out the side of the head, the floppy wide-brimmed hat pulled well down over the face.

Tensing, the blood pounding in his ears, he slipped the rest of the way out of the bed and crouched down on the floor, knees drawn up to his chest as he waited.

He had taken the precaution to screw the long, bulky silencer onto the barrel of the Luger. Now he squinted along it, eyes alert, every nerve keyed up to its tautest pitch.

The gun in the other's hand dipped a little. He saw the knuckles whiten as the finger tightened on the trigger. Then the Luger jerked viciously in his hand. The faint plop preceded the muffled scream by a fraction of a second. There was a clatter as the gun dropped from the assassin's hand onto the thick carpet.

Carradine twisted over, came to his feet like a cat, and hurled himself forward over the bed. The man at the window had half-turned. Whether to try to reach the gun lying on the floor at his feet or to jump out onto the narrow balcony outside the window, it was impossible to tell. Carradine hit him just above the knees, head pulled well down, his arms going around the other's legs, holding him firmly in a tight grip. Staggering, the other fell against the wall. There was a muffled curse. Then a down-swinging arm struck Carradine on the side of the neck.

The blow stunned him for a moment. He felt his senses slipping away and forced himself to his knees. His grasp around the other's legs had slipped a little and the man had wrenched himself free, moving back slightly. Out of his tear-blurred vision, Carradine saw the foot drawn back; the heavy toecap, glistening a little in the moonlight, poised to kick him in the face. Desperately he jerked his head to one side as the shoe came at him from the dimness, aimed for his temple. Had the blow landed, it would have killed him outright. As it was, his sudden movement took the other unawares, throwing him off balance.

Only the wall at his back prevented the assassin from falling. He half-dropped to his knees and lunged forward, fingers scrabbling for the gun on the carpet. His fingers closed over it, then opened again as Carradine stamped down on the back of his hand. The man uttered a strangled yelp. As he withdrew his hand, Carradine kicked the gun away into the far corner of the room. He felt lit with a sudden hot tongue of rage. Leaping forward, he smashed a savage blow at the assassin's exposed chin. His knuckles rasped off the granite-like flesh and as the man's hat fell off he saw the dark, malignant eyes staring up at him, lips drawn back in an animal snarl over the broken teeth. All of the skin seemed to have been abraded off Carradine's knuckles and the other did not seem to have been too badly damaged by the force of the blow, which would have knocked out any normal man. He hammered another blow at the other, trying to jerk the man's head back so that he might deliver a sharp karate blow to the Adam's apple, sufficient to knock him out, but not to kill him. He wanted this man alive. He did not really care how much alive, just so that he could get him over to Corella and force him to talk. After that, he did not care at all what happened to him. No doubt the Head of P. had ways of getting rid of unwanted men, even here in Portugal.

A harsh, rasping roar came from the other's throat. He pushed his head forward so that it was impossible to get at his throat, then heaved upwards with a surge of superhuman strength. Carradine felt himself being carried backwards, pinned against a wall on the far side of the window. All this time the other had scarcely made a sound, even when his wrist had been smashed by the bullet from the Luger. God, thought Carradine, what sort of a man was this? How could anyone continue to fight with a broken wrist as this man was doing? Was there nothing he could do to finish the other off?

Fingers went around his throat, the thumb and forefinger pressing into the main artery. Carradine struggled desperately as he felt his strength and senses slipping away from him. He could not draw in a single breath. The pounding, raw in his head, was a gigantic sledgehammer thundering against the grey wall of his brain. He felt his tongue begin to protrude from his parted lips; felt his eyeballs bulge as the tremendous pressure increased. His arms hung limply at his side. Through his blurred vision he saw the other's grinning features; saw the look of diabolical triumph in the dark eyes.

The look suddenly brought a burst of

anger into Carradine's mind. His reaction was purely instinctive. Spreading both his arms wide, he stiffened his hands and brought them swinging in together with all of his strength. He felt the shudder along his muscles as the sides of his hands struck the other simultaneously on each side of the abdomen. Even through the thick protection of the man's clothing, the blow was sufficient to bring a *whoosh* of pain bursting from his thick, rubbery lips. His eyes squeezed themselves shut and the stranglehold on Carradine's throat loosened a little. Not much, but enough for him to suck down air to the depths of his lungs. Sweat was a cold dampness on his face and along his back. He was aware of the chill touch of the carpet on the soles of his feet, and the trembling in his legs as he forced himself upright. For several seconds he was unable to move. Indeed, it was the killer who was able to move first. He was half-bent over, retching a little from the force of the double blow. Somehow, he straightened up. The colour had drained from his face and there was a new expression there. The look of triumph had vanished and in its place was one of murderous anger and cunning.

Carradine guessed that it was now going to be a battle to the finish. The other's orders had evidently been to kill him and this was just what the man intended to do. If only he hadn't dropped the Luger somewhere during the fight. If only he had killed the other when he had had the chance. Getting information from this man was nothing if he wasn't around to hear it.

He felt a momentary anger at himself as he forced his brain to clear. Out of the edge of his vision he saw the other's hand come ringing back at him in a karate blow and put up an arm to ward it off. The impact almost broke his arm. Gasping with the pain, he swung round, pivoting swiftly, and jabbed with stiffened fingers at the other's belly, just below the breastbone. The other uttered an explosive gasp and swayed back, out of the open window and onto the balcony. Swiftly, Carradine flung himself forward after the other. There was the salty taste of blood in his mouth and his arm, where the gunman's bullet that afternoon had seared along it, was beginning to pain him once more. But he was scarcely aware of these pains; all that concerned him now was to finish off the other before he was killed himself.

The assassin reeled back against the low rail of the balcony. His hand was in the pocket of his coat. A second later, the moonlight glittered off naked steel. Holding the knife in front of his body, the other went into a low crouch, balanced on the balls of his feet like a wrestler.

As Carradine came rushing forward the other lunged, thrusting the blade of the knife out directly in front of him, aiming for Carradine's chest. Only his instinctive reaction and the long months of rigid training in this kind of fighting saved Carradine then. Even as the tip of the knife reached out for him, he swayed slightly to one side, twisting his body. The knife touched his ribs through the thin cloth of the pyjamas. He fell it glide along his skin. The other's face was fiendish in the yellow moonlight.

Now there was a need to hurry. He

doubted his ability to overcome this man with the knife if the fight continued much longer. The other had the edge on him and it was no longer a question of taking the man alive so that he might be forced to give them some new information. It was a question of saving his own life. He slashed sideways with the side of his hand as the other came forward again. The blow connected, more by luck than judgement. With a strangled cry the other fell back, his face working horribly as he struggled to draw air down into his straining lungs, the muscles of his throat temporarily paralysed by the force of the blow. The eyes began to flicker upward. But he still had his grip on the long-bladed knife. There was a growing numbness in Carradine's body but he knew he had to move. If he once stopped and gave the other the chance to recover, it would mean the end.

Another vicious slash and the other's head fell back. The knife slipped from his fingers and dropped with a tinkling clatter onto the balcony. Before he could recover, Carradine drew back his foot and kicked at the man's groin. The face changed in the moonlight. The heavy muscles relaxed, the jowls drooping, the eyes opened wide, the whites showing as the pupils rolled up, almost vanishing completely. For a second, the other hung there. Then, before Carradine could make a move to save him, the head and shoulders, the whole of the upper half of his body, tilted over the low rail of the balcony and slipped upwards into space, the legs lifting from the floor. Carradine had no idea how it happened. With an effort, he reached out to try to grab the thick-set legs as they tipped like a see-saw, balanced for a moment in the air. Then the other was gone, tipping backward into the night.

Carradine half-walked, half-fell to the rail and peered over, staring down into the moonlit courtyard below the balcony. The other's body lay spread-eagled on the stone, arms and legs flung wide. His upturned face gleamed dully in the moonlight. The heavy coat was open, spread out around him like a parachute. A little incongruous thought went through Carradine's mind. For all the world, the other looked like a parachutist who had fallen without his chute opening properly. He gave a deep sigh and stood up on his shaking legs. His hands were trembling where they gripped the cold metal of the rail. Shaking his head in an effort to clear it, he brushed his hand over his sweating face. The night air laid a chill finger along his spine where the perspiration was evaporating rapidly. Now that it was over, he felt the burn along his arm and there was the warm stickiness of blood on his chest.

He fumbled with the pyjama jacket and looked down at his own body. There was a thin crimson cut across his ribs where the razor-sharp blade of the knife had cut into the skin. A tiny smear of blood was oozing slowly from it. Wearily, he went back into the room, found the two guns, picked up his own and thrust it under the pillow. He stared down at that one which the other had been carrying. It was a Walther, equally deadly. Taking out the magazine, he extracted the bullets. In the moonlight he turned them over in his fingers and saw with a faint sense of surprise that each had been nicked on the tip to give them a dum-dum effect. Had one of them hit him, it would have splayed open his body, tearing a great gaping hole in him. Wiping the sweat off his forehead, he told himself that these people were taking no chances with him.

Gathering saliva in his mouth, he forced himself to swallow thickly. The life was beginning to return to his body now and he found himself able to think more clearly. A moment later, he heard the movement down in the courtyard beneath his window. So something had been heard! Now that the body had been discovered there would naturally be an inquiry and the police would have to be brought in. He knew that the hotel management would do everything in its power to hush things up and avoid a scandal. That was the last thing in the world they could afford, especially during the height of the tourist season.

He waited patiently, sitting in the chair beside the window. Three minutes later there came an urgent but discreet knock at the door. Getting to his feet, he walked over to it, unlocked it and threw the door open. The hotel manager and the night porter were standing there. The two faces, white in the light from the corridor, stared directly at him. Their mouths were open and their eyes glinted faintly.

'I fear there has been an accident, Mr. Carradine,' said the manager, wringing his hands in deep apology for having woken him. 'I was hoping that you would be able to help us. A man is — '

'Lying in the courtyard under my window,' Carradine said dispassionately. He nodded. 'I think you had better come inside.'

The other hesitated. He said: 'I have already telephoned the police. It is necessary, I regret, but in a case such as this, they have to be told at once. Perhaps it would be better if you could come down to my office. They'll want to ask you a few questions. Nothing much, just routine, you understand?'

'Certainly I'll come,' said Carradine quietly. 'If you would just give me a few minutes in which to dress.'

'Of course. The porter will bring you to my office.' Turning, the other hurried off along the corridor.

Five minutes later, Carradine was

seated in the manager's office, sipping the brandy which the other had poured out for him. 'This is very regrettable, Mr. Carradine. I cannot apologise enough for what has happened, and on your first night here. I trust that you — '

'I shall tell the police only as much as I know,' Carradine said. 'And as for what happened, I must confess that I have never seen this man before in my life. I can only assume that he was either a madman, or that it was a case of mistaken identity. I cannot imagine why anyone should want to break into my hotel room and try to kill me.'

The other spread his hands wide on the table. 'This has never happened before in the whole history of the Hotel Marrimos. I shall have a word in the ear of the police chief. He is a personal friend of mine. It may be that this man was simply a thief. Do you know if he carried a gun?'

Carradine shook his head. 'I don't think so. He had a knife. That is it there.' He inclined his head towards the knife which lay on the table in front of him.

The manager gave a visible shudder as

he switched his gaze to the weapon, then looked back to Carradine. 'The police may recognise the man as a known criminal. If that is the case, as it may well be, I would appreciate it if — '

Carradine smiled. 'You may rest assured that I shall not speak further of the matter. If he was a thief, and he has taken nothing, he must have been surprised when I interrupted him. I think he was possibly trying to make his getaway when he tripped and fell over the balcony rail. It is extremely low.'

'I agree.' There was relief in the other's voice.

Carradine could see that he had already made up his mind that the man was a thief who had been disturbed in the act and had fallen to his death accidentally over the rail. It was the best explanation he could salvage from the circumstances, the one which he would stick to for the sake of the reputation of the hotel. Somehow, Carradine had the feeling that the police would also accept this explanation rather than try to look for some other, more sinister reason underlying the affair.

This indeed proved to be the case. The two officials who arrived less than ten minutes later listened politely to Carradine's version of what had happened: of how he had woken to find an intruder coming into the room through the window, and how the man had climbed up to the balcony and seen the window not properly closed. The man had panicked when Carradine had woken and had pulled a knife on him, then fled when Carradine had succeeded in wrestling it from his grasp. He added that he had tried to save the other when he had run out onto the balcony, slipped and lost his balance, falling against the rail. Unfortunately there had been nothing he could do. The man had overbalanced and fallen before he had been able to reach him.

Yes, that was the knife the other had been carrying. Carradine had picked it up on the balcony.

One of the two officials picked up the knife gingerly between his fingers and thumb and examined it carefully, turning it over and over in the light. Then he laid it down again on the table. 'It is a very common type of weapon,' he said finally. 'One can buy a knife such as this in half a dozen shops in Overo. We would gain nothing from it.' He paused, looked piercingly at Carradine. 'I think you are right. The man came to rob you. Perhaps he had seen you arrive at the hotel and thought to himself, here's a rich Englishman on holiday. It would have been comparatively easy for him to discover which room you had been given. Do you wish to make any claim against the hotel?' The tone the other used indicated that if he did, Carradine would have to be prepared for a long, drawn-out affair which would not benefit him in the end.

'Certainly not.' He shook his head. 'Nothing was taken. I'm only sorry that he had to meet such an end.'

6

The Watchdogs

It was one of those hot mornings when, by rights, the air should have been easy and shimmery with the heat of the sun. Instead it was like wine, so clear that details several miles along the coast could be seen with pinpoint clarity. To Carradine, standing near the pool waiting for Veronique, the scene had something poignant and dramatic about it all. It brought memories flooding back into his mind which he had thought to be long forgotten.

The touch of the hot sand between his toes made the memories sharper still. Those days had flown by so swiftly so that, looking back, it seemed as if they had happened to another person and he had been merely an outside spectator watching the events. Pre-war days in the thirties when the pace of living had seemed so slow that it would not have been recognisable, or understood by the youth of today.

Music came to him across a stretch of sand. From time to time the shrill shouts of children passing a brightly coloured beach ball from one to the other sounded above the lilting melody. How long ago since he had been in their shoes? He rubbed a hand on his cheek. When one was a child, a week seemed like an eternity. But once the age of twenty-one was passed, almost as if that number of years held a magic quality, the time fled so swiftly that a whole year was gone before one noticed it.

Tiny crabs scuttled away across the last stretch of sand before the water, moved into the sea and were lost to sight, leaving only a faint drifting line of slowly settling sand to give an indication of their passage beneath the clear water.

He lifted his gaze out beyond the clear blue stretch of water, to where the curving promontory curled in from the north, and then swung his eyes a little almost due west to where the island he had noticed the day before humped its dark bulk from the sea. What secrets lay out there, if any? he wondered. There was that same icy feeling in his mind that he had felt the previous night when that long beam of moonlight on the floor of his room had begun to widen.

Maybe this was only a hunch; maybe there would be nothing there but wild, empty rock covered with the droppings of the birds, and the birds themselves forever circling the cliffs, scolding him with weird cries if he tried to clamber onshore. But the nagging germ of suspicion in his mind would, he knew, give him no peace until he had ascertained all of this for himself. There had been too many occasions in the past when a similar hunch had led him on a dangerous manhunt which had ended with someone being killed.

Was the same thing going to happen again? A small easterly offshore breeze was beginning to ripple the surface of the water. He turned and let his glance wander over the rest of the beach to either side of him, looking for the girl. The hotels that stood a little way back from the sand looked newly painted, almost glaringly so in the bright sunlight, and the gaily coloured umbrellas which had been set out in the grounds fronting the long strip of beach made vivid splashes of blue and red and gold against the background of flowers and blue sky.

Over to his right he watched the steps leading down from Corella's beach house. There was no one in sight. He glanced at the watch on his wrist. It was five past ten. She was already five minutes late and he had gained the impression before that she was a girl who prided herself on her punctuality. Still, he thought inwardly, it was a woman's privilege to keep a man waiting.

He was still watching the distant flight of stone steps when he heard the light step behind him and whirled quickly, instinctively. There was a quiet laugh.

'You're still a trifle too nervous, Steve,' said the girl softly.

'Sorry. I wasn't expecting you to come from that direction.'

'I heard what happened at the hotel last night. The news is that it was a thief who fell from the balcony outside your window. Was it one of their men?'

'I've no doubt about it,' said Carradine casually. 'He had a gun, but I didn't let the police or the hotel manager know that, otherwise there might have been some very awkward questions for me to answer. Besides, it would have drawn attention to myself and that is the last thing I want at the moment.'

She laid a hand on his arm. 'I understand. Now you know why I want you to be very careful. Your coming here seems to have stirred them up into a real frenzy. They must think that you are a very dangerous man.'

'I take that as a compliment,' he said, smiling. 'In a little while, they will discover just how dangerous. I have a serious aversion to anyone stealing into my room at night with the intention of taking a pot-shot at me while I'm asleep. Now, how did you manage with the equipment and the boat?'

'I have it all ready,' she said. She turned and ran off over the sand towards the sea. Her suntanned body gleamed in the sunlight as she reached the boat drawn up on the sand and plunged into the water beside it. Small waves curled in lazily from the larger breakers further out to sea. The foam hissed a little, bubbles bursting in the sand as the water moved slowly back each time the sea withdrew a little way. Carradine eyed the boat. It was larger than he had expected and there was an outboard motor, together with a sail now furled and laid on the bottom. He noticed the two sets of diving equipment, oxygen tanks gleaming with the dull sheen of matt-black paint.

He looked sharply at the girl. 'Why did you bring two sets of skin-diving equipment?' he asked. 'I thought I made it clear that I would be going out to the island alone.'

'Don't be silly. I know my way around the island, probably better than anyone else in Overo.'

Carradine knit his brows as he stared down at her upturned face. 'You've been out to the island?' he asked incredulously. 'Then why didn't you tell me yesterday evening? If you know that there is nothing there, then we — '

She shook her head very slowly. 'I used to go there when I was a little girl; used to take a boat out on days like this and not come back until the evening. But a lot could have happened since then. That was all more than twelve years ago.'

'I see.' He threw a swift glance in both directions along the beach. It was virtually deserted. There were several people lying or sitting beneath the coloured umbrellas two hundred yards away, but no one seemed to be taking any notice of the girl and himself. 'Let's go take a look,' he said quickly.

The engine burst into life as he pulled on the rope. Within minutes they were heading out to sea. The rocky headland loomed up on the starboard bow, drifted past them and fell behind. Seated in the stern, Carradine relaxed, legs stretched out in front of him, eyes on the girl. She seemed quite composed, her features calm, eyes looking out to sea. What was going on in her mind at that moment? he wondered. Was she really as calm and collected as she tried to appear? He remembered the way in which she had kept her head when those two thugs had attempted to kill them the previous day. A girl like this was well worth having around in an emergency.

He swept the boat in a gentle curve. He had laid the powerful binoculars he had brought with him in the bottom of the boat. Now he picked them up and scanned the island with their enhanced vision.

The nearer shore was rocky with very few landing places, even for a boat as small as this. A sheer rock wall lifted from perhaps seventy feet from the sea along most of the beach, and judging from the way the water was churned to foam at that point, he guessed that there were vicious undertows there which could drag a man down into the green depths, giving him little chance to get free.

He could see no sign of human habitation. Thousands of birds wheeled around the cliffs, lifting and falling in the great clouds. He scanned the rugged skyline and then lowered the binoculars with a very faintly audible sigh.

'Nothing?' asked the girl.

He shook his head. 'No sign of life apart from the birds. That counts for nothing, of course. If there is anyone there, it stands to reason they wouldn't show anything on this side of the island where it could be spotted from the mainland.'

'There are very few places where you can land. Most of it is barren rock, lifting sheer out of the water — not even a metre of shingle where you could pull up a boat.'

'I don't intend to take the boat anywhere near the island. We may be under observation right now. If there is anyone there, the chances that they are connected with these attacks on my life are good. They have been alerted now. They'll keep watch.'

'Hence the skin-diving equipment,' murmured the girl.

He nodded. Glancing down, he peered into the clear blue depths alongside the boat. He could see for quite a distance down where the rippling sunlight penetrated the water. A shoal of tiny fish swam into view, clustered themselves together abruptly and then were away, a shimmering shoal of silver and bronze vanishing beneath the boat.

When he judged that they were still far enough from the island to be unrecognisable even through binoculars, but near enough to reach it underwater, he stopped the engine. At once there was a smooth, oily feel of deep water around them, the boat swaying up and down in the swell. The waves lapped softly against the bows.

'Are you sure I can't come with you?' pleaded Veronique. 'I know the island; you don't. And besides, you don't know how many of the enemy you might run into there.'

'That's precisely why I don't want to take you with me. That, and the fact that we can't simply leave the boat drifting helplessly out here. Anyone on those cliffs would soon spot that something was wrong and there would be a welcoming committee waiting for us when we arrived. Now be a good girl, Veronique, and trust me. That's all I ask.'

She pouted for a moment, then nodded

her head very slowly. 'Very well. But do be careful, Steve. If you don't return in an hour, I shall head back for the mainland and get my father to bring help.'

'All right.' He strapped on the heavy oxygen tanks and wriggled his shoulders a little to ease the straps into a more comfortable position. The mask and face-piece presented no problem. There was a long-bladed sheath knife at his waist and a spear-gun which fired explosive-driven harpoons a distance of more than two hundred yards underwater. There was no point in taking a gun; it was very unlikely that it would fire properly after being in the water at such a depth and for so long a time.

The girl watched him as he strapped on the various pieces of equipment. She was quiet and very serious, helping him now and again, but for the most part simply watching without saying a word. When he was ready, with the rubber flippers on his feet, he moved to the side of the boat away from the island.

He lifted his hands to pull down the goggles over his eyes, but the girl stood up, came right up to him, took his face in her two hands and pulled it down to her own, kissing him hard and passionately.

'That's just a reminder so that you'll come back to me,' she said fiercely.

He looked down into the beautiful face for a long moment, his gaze searching her eyes. Then he smiled faintly. 'I'll be back, Veronique. Just you stick around and see. Remember, if you see any boat coming out from the island, get away from here back to the beach. I don't want them to catch you.'

'I'll keep my eyes open.'

He nodded and pulled the goggles over his eyes after first wetting them with sea-water to prevent them from steaming up with the warmth of his flesh when he put them on. He placed the face-piece firmly over his mouth and nostrils and moved clumsily to the side of the boat, pausing there for a moment with the harpoon gun held tightly in his right hand, then dropped into the sun-glittering depths.

There was a momentary bubbling of water in his ears, then no sound at all except for the pounding of his own heart. The blueness and then the green closed in around him. He could still make out the shimmering net of sunlight that struck downward through the water all about him: now it seemed quite different from how it had looked when he had been on the surface, looking down at it. It was as if his entire body was being bathed in the golden green. A swarm of fish flashed across his vision. He began to swim strongly in the direction of the island.

Had there been anyone watching him from that expanse of cliff? If so, had they seen him dive overboard? He tried to put the feeling of apprehension out of his mind. Even if anyone had seen him dive into the water they would have no way of knowing who it was. There must be hundreds of people who went skin-diving in the bay during the long summer months. No reason why anyone should attach any particular importance to him.

He enjoyed the sensation of swimming unhampered through the cool green water. Multicoloured fish were everywhere. Once he caught a glimpse of a small man-o'-war, the long, slender, whip-like tentacles hanging down from the bloated body in the water near the surface. He stayed well clear of it. These creatures, even the smaller ones, had been known to give a very bad sting.

The minutes passed. How far was he from the island now? On the boat he had reckoned that ten minutes should see him within striking distance of the sheer cliff. Down here, in the blue-green dimness where time seemed to have no meaning, it was impossible for him to guess how many minutes had elapsed since he had dived off the side of the boat into the water.

Lifting his head, he peered up towards the surface some thirty feet above him. There was still sunlight streaming down through the shifting, rippling waves, so he had still not swum into that area of water which lay in the sun-thrown shadow of the island. That was perhaps the only way he would know that he was close to his destination, when the sunlight faded in the shadow of the cliffs. He debated whether to break the surface and risk a quick look about him, then decided against it. Much too risky. A sharp pair of eyes could not possibly miss a head bobbing out of the water.

Something flashed at the edge of his vision, something below him. A larger fish perhaps? Maybe one of the sharks which were supposed to frequent these coastal waters?

He peered through the goggles, straining his eyes to pick it out again, his grip tightening convulsively on the spear-gun. What had it been? He felt sure he had not been mistaken. He went lower, down into the dimness of the depths. Nothing there. Turning his head, he glanced about him. It could have been one of the larger fish that had swum close to him out of inquisitiveness and then decided that he was nothing of interest and gone on its way. But there was that feeling of danger all about him and the crawling of the skin on the back of his shoulders, adding up to the unshakeable belief that trouble was lurking in the depths.

A moment later he had a brief glimpse of the shadow once more. It was a little behind him now, blurred and indistinct, but it had not looked like a fish. Moving easily, using powerful thrusts of his legs, he moved towards the spot where he had seen it.

Carradine's body tautened. A shoal of fish streamed past. He looked again, and this time he was not mistaken. The man, dressed in a diving outfit similar to his own, also carried a spear-gun. He came swooping down on Carradine, twisting in the water, the gun lifting as he took aim. Frantically, kicking out with all of his strength, Carradine swam to one side, felt the surge as the harpoon speared through the water within an inch of his side. Now he could make out the other's face beneath the mask: the thin gash of the mouth, cruel and ruthless; the eyes staring at him from behind the goggles. The other had circled away at a safe distance and had what looked like a quiver of harpoons strapped to his back alongside the oxygen tanks. He was busy fitting another to the harpoon gun.

With the electric shock of danger searing along his veins, Carradine lifted the gun he carried and fired the deadly harpoon at his attacker. He saw it streak through the water, leaving a thin wake bubbling behind it. He felt the jar of the explosion kick against his wrists. Even as he fired, he saw the second shape just behind the first, spearing down at him. The first man had twisted as the harpoon lanced through the water towards him. Almost, he made it. Had he not been so busy fitting the second harpoon into the weapon he carried, it was possible that he would have been able to take evasive action in time. As it was, the slender harpoon skimmed over his shoulders, missing his body completely.

What happened next was totally unexpected. The man was hidden in the great boiling bubbles that seemed to burst out in all directions around him. Carradine felt the distinct thrust of a mild explosion wave hit, pushing him back through the water. Vaguely he was aware of the man's body being hurled down into the dark depths of the ocean, twisting and tumbling as it vanished from sight, a widening stream of bubbles spewing out behind him.

Several seconds passed before he realised what must inevitably have happened. The sharp, steel-tipped harpoon had merely grazed the other's back between the shoulder blades, but it had pierced one of the oxygen tanks, bursting the metal open, ripping it apart as if it had been paper as the pressure inside had been released explosively. It was as if a small bomb had burst on the man's back. Quite possibly, Carradine thought, the other had been dead long before he had reached the deeper depths of the sea. The explosion of the cylinder would have driven long, ragged pieces of steel deep into the other's back, piercing both lungs and heart with slivers of metal.

But there was little time to think about this. Already the second man was moving in, thirsting for the kill. He had seen what had happened to his companion and he was doubly wary. Carradine watched him closely, trying to gauge what was in the other's mind. It looked as if his attacker intended to remain at a safe distance and use his own harpoon gun. Carradine's skin crawled on his back. He had only the one harpoon. Now that weapon was useless. He stared down at it in his hand for a moment, then, throwing it away, watched for a second as it plummeted into the inky black depths beneath him. He wondered if he could outswim the other. It was possible, but the chances were that now they knew where he was, there would be guards waiting for him once he reached the island.

But he had to go on! He couldn't turn back now. For the first time, he felt the itching pain of the salt water on the cuts on his body. His arm gave him the most pain, stinging like fire where the deep graze caused by the gunman's bullet had not properly healed. But the pain shocked the senses back into his body and cleared his mind as nothing else could. He still had his life, and there was a chance for him if he could only get close enough to the other to use it.

Warily the two men circled each other in the dim green world. Occasionally a silver fish would dart between them and Carradine would start with a jerk, expecting to see the steel-tipped harpoon flashing across the few intervening feet towards him. His only chance was to get the other to fire at him and then go in while the man was trying to reload the spear-gun. There was a very strong possibility that the other also carried a knife and if so, he would have to act before the other could pull it from his belt. Grimly he moved around the other, not once removing his gaze from the weapon in the man's hands. He had his own knife in his hand now, the blade sending out tiny glimmers of light whenever the sunlight touched it.

The other man was getting nervous now. It was apparent in his quick, jerky actions and the way he thrust his head around as Carradine dived away from him, then moved in close. Whether or not the other guessed that he was tempting him to fire off the harpoon he had ready, it was impossible to tell. But he suddenly lifted the gun sharply as if he had had enough of this man who was so deliberately taunting him. The harpoon missed Carradine by at least two feet. Without pausing to think, he swooped in on the other, the knife held tightly in his fist. He saw the startled look that flashed over the other's brutish face; saw the man drop the spear-gun and pluck at the knife in his belt.

Carradine closed with him savagely, kicking out with his feet, slashing down with his arm, aiming the point of the knife at the other's exposed chest. Recognising the closeness of death, the other left the knife where it was and put up an arm to take the downward thrust, one hand gripping Carradine's wrist, forcing his arm back.

Now that he had temporarily stopped the arm holding the knife, the other bunched his left fist and shot it straight for Carradine's face, hammering a blow at his chin. Carradine jerked his head back, kicked the other in the belly with his knee, and saw the look of agony on the face under the mask. Still the other came with his arm, fingers curled in a death grip around his wrists, trying to force the knife back, trying desperately to turn it so that it could be driven into Carradine's chest. Even while he did this, the other had swung his left arm once more. This time his fingers were clawed.

With a start, Carradine realised what

the other was trying to do. He was seeking to grab the face-piece, to tear it from Carradine's mouth. Then he would have him utterly at his mercy. Unable to breathe, Carradine would drown within a couple of minutes at the most.

Automatically, Carradine fought with the other. Exerting all of his strength, he gradually forced the man's arm back until the tip of the knife was less than an inch from the man's exposed throat. The wide, staring eyes looked at him from behind the goggles, utterly devoid of any expression. The hairy chest was heaving with the exertion. Carradine knew that this was not the time for any of the Queensberry rules. The other was a dirty fighter, struggling for his life; it was going to be one or the other now, a battle to the finish with no quarter asked and none given.

How much oxygen did Carradine have left in the tanks on his back? When would he have to switch into the second? Already the blood was pounding through his head like a hammer going on and on and on. He felt as if his bruised and battered body had reached its limit; that he could take no more. Around him, it seemed darker than before. Was something happening to his sight, perhaps through lack of oxygen, or were they slowly sinking to greater depths? No time to worry about that now. With a savage, superhuman effort born of sheer desperation, he jerked his right arm free of the other's octopus-like grip and swung it once more under the man's guard. He felt the knife blade go in and saw the other jerk. Then the man was dropping away from him, arms and legs flailing. He was still alive and Carradine had no way of telling whether that wound had been fatal or not.

Drawing in as much oxygen as he could until his head felt dizzy, he drifted up through the water, squinting a little as the lightness gradually returned. The water around him turned from a blue-black, through ever lightening shades of blue, then green and finally a yellow-green, with the curious rippled effect of the surface clearly visible above him. Slowly he allowed the current to drift him along as he floated upward, the knife still held in his hand. His head broke surface, the water dripping from the hair plastered on top of his skull. It remained in drops on the glass of the goggles so that he could not see very well.

But what he could see was enough. The great looming wall of the cliff was less than fifty yards away. Now that he was closer to it, he saw that it did not rise sheer out of the water as he had thought. There was a narrow thread of sand running along the base of the cliff, perhaps thirty feet wide. So there was a chance for him to get up there. He had visualised either having to swim around the island until he found a spot where he could get ashore, or alternatively scaling the sheer face of the cliff. Now it was beginning to appear as if his luck was changing for the better. He thrust the knife into the sheath and trod water for a moment as he examined the scene in front of him for any sign of life. He did not think those two characters who had attacked down there had been the only ones watching for unwelcome visitors.

He could see nothing; only the flights

of birds wheeling in great, lazy circles against the grey rock. Nothing there to explain the feeling of danger that was still in his mind.

After what he had been through under the water, there was little life left in his body. He moved his arms and legs automatically, scarcely thinking coherently of what he was doing. His one thought was to get out of the water and up onto dry land. The fact that there would almost certainly be new dangers to face there did not matter for the moment. He only knew that he would not find any rest for his weary body so long as he remained in the water.

Ten minutes later he dragged himself wearily onto the soft, warm sand and lay there, utterly unable to move for what seemed an interminable time. Gradually life and warmth returned to his limbs. Slowly he pushed himself up onto his arms, head hanging down between them, the water still running from his hair, dripping off his chin onto the sand. The thump of his heart had resumed its slower, more normal beat and he was able to take in deep breaths now without the stabbing pain in his lungs hurting him so much. His ribs felt as if they had been bruised from the battering they had received. The wound along his arm seemed hideously inflamed by the prolonged contact with the saltwater, but he knew it looked worse than it really was. These were only superficial cuts and bruises. He had come through a lot worse in his time. With an effort he pulled himself together and got to his knees, then onto his haunches, staring about him. The tall cliffs blotted out the sunlight, and the wind that sighed around the out-jutting headland a short distance away felt cold on his wet body.

Get on your feet! he told himself savagely. *There's nothing wrong with you. It was your own decision to come out here like this and you should have foreseen that someone would try to stop you*. He hadn't expected those men down there under the water though. Whoever was on this island must certainly want to make sure that no unexpected and unwanted visitors ever set foot on it.

Shaking his head in an effort to clear it, he staggered along the short stretch of beach to the out-jutting headland. Sooner or later those two men were going to be missed. Then there would be a full-scale hunt started, with men scouring the island for him. As yet he had no clear idea of what he was going to do. That depended a lot on what he found here and the chances he had of doing anything at all. One man with a knife against how many?

He reached the bottom of the cliff. As he had suspected, there was a very narrow track leading up the side, making the ascent far easier than it had appeared from a distance. Pausing, he glanced out to sea, wondering if he could signal to the girl that he was all right. By now, she might be getting worried about him and —

All thought gelled in his head. There was no sign of the boat, or of the girl. He turned his head slowly, wonderingly, as a chill swept through him. Had something happened to her? Had she been forced to take the boat back to the mainland? A host of possibilities raced in turmoil through his mind.

In the distance he could see the yellow sunlight striking on the beaches, the white walls of the hotels looming above them. But apart from a handful of yachts further along the coast, there were no other boats visible.

Worried, he began to climb the narrow staircase of stone that wound its way up the rock face in front of him, his bare feet making soft padding sounds on the rock. There was a curious mottled humming in the air that seemed to grow stronger the higher he climbed. He stared up at the sky. It was a clear, pale blue over his head but there was no plane there that he could see which would have explained the sound.

At the top of the cliff the track flipped through a jumble of huge boulders, obviously thrown up at some early geological age. He picked his way carefully through them, oblivious of the pain in the soles of his feet where needle-sharp slivers of rock cut into the flesh. Watching his footholds for loose stones that might betray his presence, he reached the further edge of the cliff and came to a point where it dipped downward again towards a valley that ran across the centre of the island, splitting it neatly into two almost equal parts. Here the humming, throbbing sound was distinctly audible, like the muffled beat of some gigantic heart hidden away beneath the ground.

That was it! It had to be the answer! The hum of machinery hidden away somewhere beneath the ground. He knit his brows in sudden thought. There had to be some way of getting inside, but where?

He eased his body carefully forward until he reached the lip of rock, peering over it down into the maze of boulders and rocks which lay beneath him. There was a kind of tough, wiry grass growing over most of the ground, obtaining a tenuous hold on life, sucking moisture from the few scant inches of earth that formed the topsoil. The breeze blowing from the east feathered the grass, making it bend before it like the green waves of the sea. The sun was warm and soothing on his cut, bruised body. There was a languorous air of utter peace and tranquillity all about him. Nothing moved but the humming insects in the air, the birds that wheeled in their flocks over his head, and that curious sound in the air as if the very atoms were being vibrated by some strange means, which told him that men were here; that the island no longer belonged only to the birds and the bees.

Flattening himself against the ground, feeling the upthrusting rocks bite into his naked body as he crawled forward, he scanned the ground that lay beneath them. It looked deserted. He took a long and comprehensive look before he drew back. There was something down there that did not fit in at all with this peaceful landscape. It was nothing very much. A less keen eye would almost certainly have missed it altogether. On the other side of the valley, almost hidden in the shadow of the rocks which rose there, were marks on the grass which could only have been made by the treads of some heavy vehicle. He wished he had the binoculars with him now just to make absolutely certain, but there seemed little possibility of him being mistaken. A tractor or something of the kind had moved across that stretch of grass, tearing it up by the roots, gouging deep into the earth, leaving the twin ruts to scar the otherwise unbroken surface.

Now how the devil had a tractor been brought here, and how could it have got over there? Unless there was an easier landing place somewhere around the island at the extreme ends of the valley, it would have to have been hauled up the sheer face of the cliff, a matter of seventy or eighty feet. Not an impossible task for present-day machinery, it was true. But why had they gone to all of that trouble? Evidently this place was not at all what it seemed on the surface.

He recalled what Corella and Veronique had told him of the foreigner who had offered to buy the island from the Portuguese government sometime before; the man whose offer had been turned down. Perhaps he had refused to take this as the last word on the matter and had moved in without permission, trusting to the fact that nobody ever came out here anyway to keep the fact secret. Carradine shrugged. The chances were that he would get away with it. Especially with a deterrent such as those two men he had encountered under the sea. They were, or had been, an excellent insurance policy against being disturbed.

7

Secret of the Island

Taking the knife from his belt, Carradine tested the blade with his thumb; then, satisfied, thrust it back again. It would be handy if he needed it. Glancing about him, he examined the terrain, trying to judge the best way of getting across to the other side of the narrow, deep-sided valley. The chances of being seen if he went directly across it were too great to risk such a move. He had to skirt around it, keeping to the cover of the rocks. It would take time and, not knowing what could have happened to Veronique, this was something he felt he had little of.

For a moment he waited, assessing angles and distances, then moved off to his right. The air was cool among the rocks, drying his body. He ran his fingers through his salt-matted hair, keeping his head low as he moved, running wherever possible, the breath rasping hard and cruel in his throat. He had no idea of what he was letting himself in for, but the eternal *thump, thump* of the engine or whatever it was sounded like a heartbeat in his ears and urged him on, telling him more plainly than words that whatever it was that was going on here, it was something he had to get to the bottom off. Something that was to work against the Western Alliance.

Nothing moved in the murmuring stillness all about him. Half an hour later he reached the far side, moving cautiously towards the spot where he had seen the tyre marks in the grass. They were there, just as he had seen them from the far side of the valley. Bending, he examined them carefully. They were gouged deeply into the soil and here and there, where the tyres had run over one of the outcroppings of rock, it had been smashed and splintered, indicating something of a very heavy weight. It looked more like a tank than a tractor, he decided finally.

Getting to his feet, he followed the tracks, keeping well in to the side of the cliff. The sun was almost at the zenith now and there were very few long shadows. The heat rolled at him from the valley and down from the rocks above his head; rolled in great invisible waves. He felt the sweat start out on his body again. The palms of his hands were slippery with it and it dripped into his eyes from his forehead. Whenever he brushed it away the salt on his skin burned into the flesh, leaving it raw and tender.

He blundered into the opening in the rock almost before he was aware of its existence. One minute he was following the tracks in the grass and the next they had swerved sharply to the right in front of him, down into the gaping mouth of the cave; the broad rocky overhang threw enough shadow there to prevent the opening from being easily discernible even by anyone standing within a few feet of it.

Instinctively he drew back, pressing his body hard against the rock, holding his breath tensely. The panting whine that was superimposed on the background hum of machinery tore at his ears. It was a shrill, almost unbearable sound that occasionally touched subsonics, which almost tore his eardrums apart. He moved further away from the opening, his mind whirling.

God, but they must have something really tremendous down there. But what was it?

Gently he eased the knife from his belt and moved away from the rock, edging forward. The faint swishing sound seemed to come from directly above him. He jerked himself back and lifted his head to peer up into the blue mirror of the sky. He had a quick impression of something snake-like that hurtled down on him. Then his arms were pinned savagely to his sides as the rope tightened about his middle. The knife dropped quivering into the dirt near his foot. The first breath of real fear stirred the hairs at the back of his neck. A few small stones rattled down the slope as the man at the end of the rope clambered down.

Exerting all of his strength, he tried to force the rope away from his body so that he could slip his arms free, but the other had jerked it so tightly that it was impossible for him to budge it. The rope merely tightened more deeply into his salt-caked skin. After a few moments he was forced to give up the attempt.

'That is much better,' said the man who dropped lightly to the ground a few feet away. 'You will only make things much worse for yourself if you try to struggle.'

There was a noticeable accent to the other's voice. Russian? Czech? One of those countries, Carradine thought.

'Now see here,' he said blisteringly. 'Just what is the meaning of this? I was told in Overo that this island was government property; that it was a wild bird sanctuary and that I could have permission to land here and look around. Then you attack me with this without any warning or explanation and — '

'Quiet!' snapped the other harshly. He jerked on the rope and it tightened a little more, crushing Carradine's chest still further, making it difficult for him to draw air down into his lungs.

A moment later two other men stepped

out of the opening in the rocks. The guns in their hands were levelled on Carradine's chest. He didn't like the smiles on their faces as they stared at him with deadpan expressions in their eyes.

'Come on forward,' said one of them tautly. 'Hurry it up. We don't have all day to wait for you.'

Carradine said stiffly, 'I shall report this action to the Portuguese government on my return. It is outrageous that a visitor should be treated in this fashion. Had I known that the island was private I would never have come here, but I was assured by the police in Overo that it was uninhabited, and also government property.' He hoped that this veiled reference to the police authorities in Overo would prompt them to think twice about him. Whatever happened, they must not know who he really was and why he was there.

The smile on the taller man's face widened. He shook his head. 'We have no dealings whatever with police in Overo,' he said smoothly. 'We do not bother them and they stay away from the island.'

'Meaning that they don't know you are

here?' Carradine said innocently.

'Meaning nothing,' said the other sharply. He stepped forward and jabbed the barrel of the gun into Carradine's stomach. The pain was exquisite. For a moment he thought he was going to be sick. It was only by a tremendous effort of will that he managed to hold it down.

'Now get inside and remember — the first move you make that I don't like, you'll get a bullet in the back of the knee.'

It was not a warning but a cold statement of fact. Carradine moved forward. There was nothing else left open to him. Without the knife he had no chance at all.

'Don't you think you can remove these ropes?' he said harshly as they stepped into the rocky chasm that led down into the bowels of the earth.

'We will consider that later,' was the laconic reply. 'In the meantime, you stay tied up, Mr. Carradine.'

Carradine felt his heart sink momentarily. So they knew who he was. At least it told him that he was on the right track. He was on the point of asking what they had done with the girl, then bit the question back. There was just a chance, the barest possibility, that she had not been taken by anyone from the island; that she was still free, maybe warning her father. The less these people knew of her, the better.

The cavern seemed to have been hewn out of the solid rock by natural, rather than artificial, means. Although in places it looked as though nature had been helped a little. There were deep gouges along the walls where machinery had been evidently used to widen the tunnel in places. As they walked down into the dimness, the throbbing hum of machinery became louder and more insistent in Carradine's ears.

'Some place you have here,' he said, his voice echoing back from the confining walls of the cavern.

'Shut up,' snapped the man walking close behind him.

Carradine shrugged with a show of indifference which he certainly did not feel. With an effort he forced a little of the tension out of his body; forced the aching muscles to relax. He was still alive. And these men had not shot him out of hand as he had half-expected them to do if he were caught. So long as there was life in his body, there would be a chance for him to try to turn the tables on them and find some way of getting out of here to warn the Portuguese authorities and get word back to the Chief in London. Whatever was going on, he felt sure that they would be interested to know about it.

There had been no immediate word the previous evening, according to Corella, regarding the man with the cross-shaped birthmark on his shoulder, although London had agreed to look into it and send word through if there was any definite information. Carradine had suggested that it might have been one of their own men and he did not think it would take long for them to find out if it were indeed the case.

Now the descent was becoming steeper instead of levelling off as he had anticipated. But a vague overall light showed in the distance. What the hell did all this mean? Who were these people, and what were they hiding here? What was so vitally important that they had to bury it from sight beneath an island off the coast of Portugal?

Carradine gazed about him with curious eyes, taking in everything as he stumbled forward, the three men at his back watchful for any movement he might make. But at the moment he had no intention of trying to escape. To do so now would be defeating the purpose of his being there. He had to find out what was going on before he made any attempt to get out. Besides, he knew that the man with the gun had not been fooling when he had said he would shoot him in the back of the leg. Silently he made his way forward. Carradine gathered together all of his reserves of strength and endurance.

He had no way of knowing what might lie ahead for him; what these people had in mind. But he steeled his mind against any thought of the unknown. Instead he focused his whole being on taking in every detail of the scene around him. Somehow, above all else, he must cling to the fact that there would be a chance for him to get away from here; and it was necessary that he should know everything he possibly could about this fantastic place.

'Stop!' The man immediately behind him jabbed the gun into his back to accentuate the word.

Obediently, Carradine halted. The tunnel continued ahead of them, still dipping down. One of the men stepped into view at the side of him, went over to the wall of rock and thumbed a hidden button. A section of the rock — or what appeared to be the rock, but which on closer inspection turned out to be a section of metal cunningly camouflaged as rock — slid to one side. There was an elevator set in the cliff wall. Carradine stared in surprise.

Wonder piled on wonder. The grille door slid open and there was a man standing in the elevator. Carradine, his hands held tightly to his side by the rope, was thrust forward, the three men crowding in on his heels. The door hissed shut, sliding with very well-oiled smoothness that indicated constant use.

God, but this set-up was becoming

more and more fantastic every moment. During the war, in England, he knew that places like this had been built below ground to protect them from the endless Luftwaffe raids. Churchill had had a place somewhere in London, he recalled, where he went whenever the raids were at their height. But to have constructed something of this magnitude must have taken thousands of pounds, if not millions.

The man at the door pressed the buttons. They drifted downward. Standing there, Carradine tried to estimate the distance travelled. The elevator sighed gently to a stop, the door was opened and he was thrust forward. Blinding light played over his face and he screwed up his eyes in automatic reflex. For several seconds it was not possible to see anything beyond that terrible glare of actinic light.

Gradually his vision returned to normal. There were two corridors leading off into the distance. One of them, to his left, opened out about thirty yards away into a vast underground chamber. There were machines, gleaming metal instruments, lining one side of it; what looked like computers and a long control panel. Something in the middle reminded Carradine of a radar panel, with a finger of green light endlessly circling the face. Hell, what a set-up this was, but what was the purpose behind it all? Some secret submarine base, based here so the enemy might strike at British and American shipping without warning, using the shorter sea route to get astride the Atlantic shipping lanes? It seemed a very distinct possibility. Nobody would think of looking here for anything like that. He remembered the gigantic underground pens which the Nazis had built during the war. They must have been on this sort of scale.

Not only that, but a place such as this was a veritable fortress. It would be virtually impossible to get at it to destroy it, short of blowing up the entire island with something like a hydrogen bomb.

'This way,' said the man at his back. He motioned to Carradine to move along the other corridor to the right. Reluctantly, Carradine tore his gaze from the scene in the vast chamber and made his way along the short, straight corridor. There were doors opening off it to either side. Most of them were closed, but from behind one or two of them he heard the faint grinding hum of more machinery.

The man halted at the door at the very end and knocked twice with the butt of his pistol. There was a momentary pause and then a light flickered on over the door. The other opened it, went inside and motioned Carradine to follow him.

Cautiously, not knowing what to expect, Carradine stepped through. A pale glow illuminated the room and as he stared about him in bewilderment, he stopped dead in his tracks. He might have stepped off the lift at one of the most expensive hotels in the heart of London and into the best suite. The furniture had been tastefully chosen, the floor was closely carpeted with a maroon thick-laid carpet, and there were two carefully shaded fluorescent lights set close to the ceiling so that they cast a cool blue light without any shadows.

There was a broad mahogany desk at the far side of the room with a tall, shiny intercom at one end of it. The chair was the kind a top executive in one of the biggest companies might have, and the man seated in it looked every inch a prosperous businessman. He got to his feet as Carradine shuffled forward, moved around the side of the desk and held out his hand. 'Mr. Carradine. It is so good to see you, even though our meeting has been a trifle delayed.'

'I'm afraid I — '

'My name is François duCann. You have heard of me.' It was more of a statement of fact than a question and Carradine suppressed the faint start of surprise, merely inclining his head in silent acknowledgement.

'Good.' The other waved him to a chair, sat down himself, produced a slender gold cigarette case and offered it to him. Carradine selected one and picked up the solid silver light from the desk, drawing the smoke deeply into his lungs. The other was up to something with this hail-fellow-well-met type of welcome. He stiffened his senses, watching the man warily.

'I also know quite a lot about you, Mr. Carradine. I know who you work for and why you are here.' He smiled, blowing smoke into the air through his pursed lips. 'I do not, of course, mean the concern which is shown on your passport. That would not fool anyone, as you no doubt realise.'

'It sometimes helps,' Carradine said softly.

'Perhaps. But as you see, I know so much about you that there is no need for me to ask questions, to cajole you into talking about yourself. You are here because the British Secret Service has been wondering a little about certain rumours they may have heard from their agents inside Portugal. So they send a man out to see what is going on — whether there is any grain of truth in these stories; whether they are merely the figments of some newspaperman anxious to get himself a story.'

'And all the time, the little grain of truth in them is something far bigger than even the Portuguese government has guessed at.'

'How right you are.' The other was quite pleased. He was supremely confident in himself, believing that he had

Carradine so utterly at his mercy that any thought of escape was completely out of the question. 'You will have seen a little of what we have here when you came in. Quite impressive, is it not? But that is only one part of everything down here under the island. It is what you have not seen that is so important.'

'And no doubt all of this has been financed by the Soviets?'

The other spread his hands expressively on top of the desk. 'But naturally. You do not think for one moment that the Portuguese government would be able to provide either the funds or the technology to create anything like this?' There was an undeniable note of pride in his voice. Carradine had typed the other quite accurately. The man was an egomaniac. He was so puffed up with his own importance there was just the chance his human failing might be used against him.

'Are you in command of it all? Just where does Varandashky fit into all this?'

For a moment the mask of confident assurance slipped from the other's features. Then he shrugged. 'So you have heard of Varandashky?'

'Naturally. To be quite honest with you, it is him I am after. I had heard nothing of you until I met your daughter on the plane from London.'

'I heard all about that from Solitaire. She was one of my reserve weapons in case my men, or your own curiosity, failed.'

Carradine made no comment, staring at the other through the smoke from his cigarette.

After a pause the other smiled, saying: 'As you see, it was your own curiosity which trapped you in the end, just as I was sure it would.'

'How do you know it trapped me?' Carradine asked. 'All you know is that I am here. You seem to have jumped to the conclusion that I came alone; that no one knows where I am. I'm afraid that nothing could be further from the truth. There are several very important people who know exactly where I am, and also what to do if I do not return to Overo by nightfall. You say that you know everything about me. Then you also know that

I do not walk into situations which are so obviously loaded with danger without taking precautions first.'

'I see no reason to doubt you, Mr. Carradine,' said the other easily. He did not seem to be put out in the least by this remark. 'But even when you do not return, there will be no trouble as far as I'm concerned. There is no possibility at all of them ever finding you. I must admit that we made a foolish mistake a year ago when one of your agents started snooping around the island just when we were building the site. He managed to bribe one of my most trusted men to help him. Naturally I could not allow this to go on. Had my orders been carried out to the letter, those men would have left no trace and there would have been no repercussions, no enquiry. But someone bungled the job and their bodies were washed ashore a couple of days later. But as you have probably discovered for yourself, the police do not concern themselves with these matters when there is a quite logical explanation. I've provided them with such an explanation and they are quite satisfied. As for you, I believe you came ashore after swimming underwater to the island from a boat out in the bay. You will be presumed drowned when you do not return. These waters can be very treacherous with swift and powerful currents that can drag a man down without warning.'

'Or there are men with spear-guns to make certain that where the currents fail to do their work properly, there are always other ways of making sure that a man dies.'

'Those men were fools. They deserved to die if they could not destroy one man after taking him by surprise.' For the first time a note of anger crept into the other's voice and Carradine saw the fingers tighten on the edge of the desk, the knuckles standing out white under the flesh with the pressure he was exerting.

Carradine drew deeply on his cigarette and stared down at the glowing tip, deliberately ignoring the other's anger. 'You still haven't told me about Varandashky. What does he do around here? The paid killer, or the collector of the top scientific minds in Britain and America?'

'Something like that,' said the other with a shrug. 'He shuttles back and forth between Britain, Russia and Portugal.'

'I suppose his job is also to see that there are no mistakes here. After all, with such a large capital investment, the Russians will want to be absolutely certain that they get a just return for their money. And they can't afford word of this leaking out to the rest of the world. It would be another little Cuba all over again.'

'That will not happen, I assure you.' There was a note of conviction in duCann's voice. 'My position is such that I, too, could not afford to allow it to happen.'

'I can imagine,' said Carradine dryly. 'I suppose that you have your plans for me? What are they to be? A bullet in the back from one of your thugs — or a lead weight around the legs and a dive into the ocean?'

'Nothing so crude,' said the other. He tapped the bulky file on the desk. 'This is your official file, or rather a copy of the original, which is held in Moscow. It makes very interesting reading, believe me. It is unfortunate that you will not have the chance to peruse it. But from what is written here I see that you are no ordinary agent. The orders concerning you are that if you are ever apprehended, Moscow is to be informed immediately. They will then decide what your fate is to be and it will be up to me — or rather our friend, Varandashky, to see that the order is carried out. There will be great rejoicing in Moscow when it is learnt that you have finally been eliminated.'

'I suppose that is one of the greatest compliments they can pay to an enemy agent.'

'I would think of it that way if it is of any comfort to you in your last moments.' He glanced at his watch. 'The orders will not come through for another hour or so at least. They take their time making up their minds in a case like this. They may even ask that you be taken back to Russia where they will no doubt have questions of their own to put to you, and their own methods of loosening your tongue.' Pushing back his chair, he leaned forward, stubbed out his cigarette in the ashtray, rubbed his fingertips together, then said: 'But no doubt you would like to see what it is you are going to die for, the secret your death will help to preserve.'

'I'd be delighted.' Carradine stood up, crushed out his own cigarette and followed the other.

* * *

DuCann's lips glazed into a thin, hazy smile as he stood at the entrance to the vast underground chamber and waved an expressive arm to embrace it all. It had become immediately apparent to Carradine that his initial thought that this was a submarine pen was wrong. It was something far more than that.

'I will not bore you with the more mundane details, Mr. Carradine,' said the other quietly. 'You are an intelligent man. The foreign police of the Soviet Union underwent a radical change with the death of Stalin, and another during the crisis over Cuba. Speaking confidentially, the loss of the rocket bases in Cuba was a tremendous blow to their procedure. They had been relying on this to swing the balance of power in their favour. You can imagine the effect their climb-down had with the generals. There was quite an outcry — a discreet one, naturally. One does not question the decisions of the Praesidium without due regard to the possible consequences. But even the Praesidium must have realised that there was a general feeling of unrest among the military. Certainly the tensions built up by the siting of rocket missiles in Cuba, right on America's doorstep, created a situation that was rapidly becoming highly dangerous. Russia did not want to start an all-out nuclear war. It was recognised that if this happened, Russia would be utterly destroyed as well as America and possibly the rest of the world with them. So they looked into the whole position very carefully to see where they had gone wrong, where the fundamental mistake had been. According to the Russian psychology, whenever something fails to work out the way they think it should, then there has to be a mistake somewhere along the line. They later decided that it was because those missile sites could be spotted so easily from the air. Cuba was known to be pro-communist. The Americans knew it and it was only natural, inevitable, that they should send their spy planes over the island, taking photographs, bringing back the information.'

Carradine sucked in a deep breath. He was beginning to get the picture now — the whole stupendous picture of what was going on here, right under the noses of the Western Allies. God, London had to know about this. If anything meant life and death for millions of innocent and unsuspecting people, this was it. He stared at duCann with expressionless eyes, his face cold and tight.

'I see that you are beginning to understand,' murmured the other. 'They decided that another base had to be built, but on a much larger scale than that they had planned in Cuba. It was to be always directly under their control. They had one of their agents put in a bid for this island, knowing quite well that the offer would be refused by the Portuguese government. That was merely a blind, to ensure that they had been right in thinking that no one would be allowed take over the island. Once that was assured, then they could go ahead with their plans.'

'So here we have a great new rocket and missile site right on our own doorstep, and the balance of power has once more been shifted in favour of the Russians; only nobody knows about it but them.'

'That is only part of the truth, Mr. Carradine.' The other seemed to be enjoying himself immensely. Carradine had not been wrong about this man's egomania.

'You mean that there is more?' he asked, prompting the other.

'Of course. Here, we are almost on the line of the orbital trajectories of the American space shots and moon probes. You realise how vitally important it is to Russia that they should win the space race and be the first with a manned rocket on the moon. We have tracking devices here which can pick up the initial lift-off stages of every rocket the Americans fire. We know within seconds of these firings. There are rockets here with nuclear warheads which can be used to intercept and destroy any of their space shots. We can also put up our own satellites into orbit, and all that crosses most of the United States. These will be equipped with the latest cameras and television devices enabling us to photograph every part of that country — a task which has its complications when we have tried to rely on rockets fired from a site in Russia.'

Carradine felt a shiver go through him. What in God's name had he got himself into? He had come here expecting to find some Red group, maybe trying to build themselves up into something big, ready to move in if there was another war. And instead he had stumbled upon this, the biggest thing since the Cuban crisis; maybe a whole heap bigger. Oh God, he had to get word of this out. He had fluttered into the web to bring the spider out into the open so that he could be recognised, only to find it was a tarantula he was dealing with, the grandpappy of them all!

DuCann coughed delicately. 'I can see that you are suitably impressed by what you have seen and been told. I regret that there is not time to show you the missiles themselves. They have all been brought here by a submarine on board one of the *Sverdlovsk* cruisers during a goodwill visit to Portugal and Spain. No one suspects anything. By the time they do, it will be far too late.' He smiled at Carradine. 'Do you think that your life means anything compared with a plan such as this? Or even my life, precious as it is to me?'

Carradine said nothing. He had a momentary memory of that room in London, with the chief telling him that there was evidence that Varandashky was in Overo in Portugal; that he probably had a ring there for smuggling scientists and vital scientific information from the West into Russia. Carradine was to take the plane the next day and try to find out what it was all about. So he had taken the plane, had enjoyed an hour's conversation with a very beautiful girl, had met another at the airport in Lisbon, and had been shot at on the way to Overo. But all the time he had thought that there was nothing more than a Red smuggling ring for obtaining information from Britain and getting it back to Russia. Now he had found out the secret which had been kept so well hidden from the outside world, and there seemed no hope for him at all. It was a secret he would take with him to the grave, wherever that might turn out to be.

God, what a bloody fool he had been. He had done exactly what the Chief had warned him against: completely underestimated the opposition. Now he was paying the price for his stupidity. He set his teeth as two men came forward from the shadows. They both carried rifles.

'I regret that I cannot allow you any freedom until the final orders are received from Moscow,' duCann said, his voice very soft. 'But you must realise my position. You have been responsible for the death of at least four of my men and I cannot afford to take any chances.'

For a moment the thought of action was strong within Carradine's mind. He gauged the distance to the other and wondered briefly if it would be possible for him to reach the man and use him as a shield against the others, as his guarantee of getting out of there alive.

But duCann had taken the precaution of moving well away from him and the two men had their fingers on the triggers of their weapons, the safety catches already clicked off, ready to fire at his first move. Besides, as duCann had said so truthfully, his own life was of little importance compared with the plan which was being put into action here. There was no doubting that these men would shoot, even if it meant killing duCann in the process.

'Take him away,' said duCann softly.

One of the guards moved up behind Carradine, reached out and took hold of his arm, his fingers curled like an iron band around the bicep. Carradine winced as the fingers bit into his flesh. The other man stood a few feet away, the barrel of the rifle trained unwaveringly on him.

Shrugging, he allowed himself to be led along the corridor, away from the underground cavern holding its dreadful secret. He was taken back to the elevator. The door hissed shut and they moved upward this time, the distance somewhat shorter than when he had first gone down a little while before. Evidently they were still inside the mountain.

The door slid open. A rifle barrel prodded him in the back and he stumbled forward along a rough-hewn passage that led off to his right. There was little light here and the walls dripped moisture, forming into puddles on the floor. Something scurried across the dimly lit rocks and raced out of sight. Then there was another movement and Carradine caught a glimpse of malevolent red eyes that glared ferally at him from the shadows.

One of the men laughed at his reaction. 'Plenty of company for you here,' he said harshly. 'Reckon you won't be too lonely until we come to fetch you again.'

He pushed open a heavy door set in the wall. Beyond it was a square cell perhaps ten feet along each side, the ceiling less than six feet from the rough floor. Bending his head, he went inside. Immediately the door clanged shut behind him. There was a small square grille set solidly in the door, edged with metal. Through it, he saw the two men walk away along the passage. Then he was left alone in the comparative darkness.

There were no benches or seats of any kind and he was forced to squat on the cold stone floor, knees drawn up to his chest. He flexed his fingers, feeling stiff and numb. His arm too, where saltwater had soaked into the burned and blistered flesh, stung atrociously. He was not in the best physical condition, he thought dully; yet he had to get out of there somehow and, without any of his usual weapons, it was not going to be easiest thing in the world. He thought longingly of the small suitcase that contained so many weapons, so many ways of getting his freedom. Now it reposed in his room at the hotel and it was beginning to look as though he would never see it, or the hotel, again.

Leaning his back and shoulder against the wall, he tried to think things out calmly and logically. Panic was fatal at this point. He had perhaps an hour in which to try to work out some way of getting out of there. Obviously he could do nothing so long as he was locked up here in this cell. Therefore it would have to be when those guards came for him, once a radio message arrived from Moscow.

He had counted the steps from the elevator to the door to his cell. Thirty-three. If he managed to walk slowly, he might string it out to a couple of minutes, certainly not more. Both men would be on their guard. DuCann would probably have picked them himself and warned them of his reputation, maybe even overdoing it a little just to make sure that there were no slip-ups.

He finally decided that his only chance would be to take one of the two men when they took him from the cell, and while one of them was closing the heavy door. If he could grab hold of a rifle, he stood a slender chance — a chance so remote that it seemed non-existent. But it was the only one he had.

8

The Loser

Later, unable to tell how much later, Carradine heard the movement inside the cell — a sound that echoed along the corridor at the end of which stood the cell in which he crouched. Gently, he eased himself to his feet. The guards were returning. He had to ensure that his limbs were not so stiff that they would not obey his will when he made his move. He rubbed his legs. They were icily cold. The air in the small cell had been chill and unmoving. There had been air conditioning throughout most of the rooms in the great cavern in the centre of the mountain, but it had clearly not been extended as far as this.

He crouched low near the door, gathering his wits and conserving his energy. Everything was going to depend on split-second timing and swift movement. Once he started, he would not be able to turn back. Raising his head cautiously, he saw the two dark shadows, curiously elongated and crazily distorted on the far wall of the corridor, long before the men who made the shadows came into view. When they did he saw that they were the same men who had escorted him there.

He drew in a deep breath, forcing his mind to ignore the pain in his arms and chest. A key rattled in the lock of the door. Getting his legs under him, he waited, every muscle and nerve in his body poised. The door creaked open on rusty hinges. One of the men lowered his head and peered inside. The other held his gun on him, standing well away from the door, alert, ready for trouble.

Carradine sighed, shrugged his shoulders and pushed himself to his feet.

'What is it now?' he said. 'More boring talk with duCann?'

'You'll soon find out for yourself,' snapped the man. He stood to one side as Carradine stepped out, stretching himself as if stiff from the long period of confinement. His only chance was to distract the others either by talking or pretending that he was in no condition to make any resistance. He stretched his arms over his head, glancing sideways at the man near the door. He was bent over the lock, fumbling with the key.

Now! It was his only chance. It would take a few seconds for the other to turn, straighten up and unsling the rifle from over his shoulder. Carradine moved forward slowly, unobtrusively, until he was level with the guard standing watchful with the gun. He rubbed his knuckles into his eyes as if he'd just been wakened from a sleep and saw the slow, sneering grin that began to form on the man's lips. Then without warning, his left arm slashed down at the other's arm just above the wrist. There was an ominous crack. The other yelped with the pain of a broken arm, dropped the gun onto the stone floor and swayed back, his other hand instinctively cradling the smashed arm.

Carradine dived for the gun on the floor. His fingers closed around the barrel and tried to pull it towards him but the guard's foot lashed out and kicked it away from him, sending it skating to the far wall. Carradine spat out an oath, kicked at the man's unprotected stomach and felt a sense of pleasure as the other reeled back, his face the colour of lead, bent double with the agony of the blow. Turning, he saw the man in the door of the cell unsling his rifle, throw off the safety catch and bring it up to cover Carradine. It was all finished now, he thought dully, the sense of defeat rushing over him. He hadn't a hope in hell of getting to the rifle on the floor in time. The man's lips twisted into an almost bestial snarl. His fingers tightened on the trigger, the rifle pointed at Carradine's legs. Another second and he would be crippled, unable to do anything.

The noise in his ear was one he had never heard before. It was like a muted hum but with a metallic twang to it that made him jerk back in surprise. The man in front of him uttered a choking cough as a palely gleaming steel shaft seemed to grow out of his chest. The rifle fell from his hands and for a long moment he stood upright, fingers curled around the harpoon as though caressing it. Then his knees buckled under him and he fell forward onto his face at Carradine's feet.

Carradine stared about him in stunned surprise. There was a movement on the far side of the corridor, where hard out-jutting slabs of rock formed deep midnight shadows.

Veronique had a second harpoon fitted to the gun and it was pointed at the man who lay moaning on the ground a few feet away, clutching at his arm.

'What do we do with that one?' she asked, her tone perfectly composed and casual.

'How on earth did you get here, Veronique?' For a moment, his relief at finding her safe overcame his surprise at seeing her there. He pulled her to him, held her close for a moment, then said quietly: 'We'll put him in the cell there where he can do no more harm.'

'Won't he cry for help?' asked the girl pointedly, as she held the door open while Carradine pushed the guard towards it.

'Somehow I doubt if he'll do that for a long time.' The man began moving past Carradine without resisting. He was evidently no fool and did not intend to commit suicide just for duCann's sake. He had seen what had befallen his companion and the look of frozen horror was still on his face as he stumbled through the low doorway. Carradine waited until he passed in front of him, then swung his hand down in a karate blow on the nape of the other's neck. He had slammed the door and locked it before the man's unconscious body had crashed to the stone floor of the cell.

Then he turned to the girl and caught her up to him again. 'Veronique. Are you sure you're all right? When I got to the island and looked at the sea and discovered that the boat had gone, I thought the worst had happened — that they had somehow caught up with you while I'd been under the water.'

She shook her head and gazed up at him, her eyes misted a little. 'I didn't wait for that to happen. As I said, I know this island better than most. I sailed the boat around to the southern tip and came ashore. There is a track there that leads directly into the valley which runs across the centre of the island. I was in the grass about half a mile away when I saw you against the cliff. I spotted the man on the ledge above you, but it was impossible to warn you and when they caught you and took you inside, I knew that I was the only one who could help you get away.'

'Why didn't you do as I told you? Take the boat back to the mainland and warn your father of what has happened?'

'I didn't think there would be time. Besides, I had no idea what they might do to you once they got you in here. Do you know that duCann has left in a launch? They have a small landing stage hidden among the rocks on the western side where they cannot be observed from the mainland. I think he's going ashore to meet Varandashky.'

'Then we have to get away from here too. Can you find your way up to the surface again?'

'I think so. I used to explore these caves and tunnels when I was young. I knew most of them then, but I've forgotten many of them now and there are some new ones too.'

While they had been talking, she had led the way to the end of the long tunnel. The door of the elevator was still open, but there was no sign of the man who operated it. Getting in, Carradine fiddled with the buttons until he found one that closed the door. Now which would take them up and which down? He pressed one experimentally. The lift began to drift downward. Damn! He waited until it came to a stop, then pressed the other, keeping his finger on it as they climbed with an agonising slowness to the surface.

When the elevator refused to go any further, he opened the door and glanced out, throwing a swift look in both directions. He recognised a long roughly hewn tunnel which ran up and down in front of the elevator opening.

'Quickly!' he said through clenched teeth. The girl needed no urging. Together they ran along the wide tunnel that sloped gently up to the surface. There was no one in sight and they reached the entrance without any sign of pursuit at their backs.

Now there was no time to talk. They

had to reach the boat and get as far from the island as possible before Carradine's escape was noticed. Very soon, when those two guards failed to turn up with him, there would be a hue and cry and the island would be swarming with men. Even when they reached the boat they might not be safe. It seemed likely that there were guns on the island which could blast them out of the water, or other fast boats which could be used to catch up with them before they reached land.

'Follow me,' called the girl thinly. He started running off along the rocks and then into the grass that stretched away in front of them for an interminable distance. The air was clean out here and he found himself able to think more clearly. The girl was managing to keep up with him as they plunged through the ankle-deep grass, leaping the numerous small streams that bubbled across the valley from one side to the other.

'How far is it to the boat?' he called.

'About a mile or so,' she answered. 'Fortunately we don't have to clamber over the rocks.'

He grinned reassuringly. 'We just keep up this pace and we'll lick them yet.' He threw a quick glance over his shoulder. In the sunlight the valley stretched away behind them, still deserted. He could just make out the opening in the rock now that he knew where to look for it. Still no sign of anyone bursting out of it.

The girl stumbled. Reaching out, he caught her around the waist, seeing the look of pain which flashed across her face.

'Are you hurt?' he asked anxiously.

'Just wrenched my ankle, that's all. I can manage all right.'

'I will help you,' he said breathlessly. 'I reckon we've got a good enough start on them now. We can ease off a little.'

They started moving again. Here and there the ground was treacherous. There were deep crevasses in the earth which they came upon unexpectedly. Any one of them would have snapped a man's ankle in two if he had fallen into it.

'What was going on down there?' Veronique asked as she leaned against him. 'I could hear a strange sound — like machinery.'

'That was only part of it,' Carradine told her. Briefly, he mentioned everything that duCann had told him when he had considered Carradine to be safely in the bag. Somehow he doubted if the other would have been so free with his information if he could know what was happening now. *We'll get you yet*, he thought savagely. *You and the whole nest of spies and enemy technicians tucked away on the very doorstep of Europe*.

There was a faint rumble behind them, rather like a peal of summer thunder rolling along the horizon. Instinctively Carradine turned. What he saw brought the tremor back into his legs and the icy chill along his spine.

Something had emerged from the wide opening in the rock — something huge glinting with the flash of moving metal in the flooding sunlight. It moved ponderously, swinging slightly on its tracks as the men on board scanned the area for a sign of them. They must have had powerful binoculars, for they seemed to pick them up at once. The mobile tractor vehicle, built along the same lines as a tank, swung round, then began to move after them, crushing everything in its path, moving extremely quickly for its bulk, coming after them with a singleness of design that froze the blood in Carradine's veins.

'What in God's name is that?' quavered the girl.

'Some kind of tank,' he said in a low, hushed voice. 'It wouldn't surprise me if they don't have a heavy gun mounted on it somewhere, or a machine-gun. Evidently I spoke too soon when I said we had a head start on them. They certainly don't mean us to get away with the information we have.'

Even as he spoke, an automatic weapon mounted on top of the tank chattered briefly as the gunner felt out their range. The shots fell short of them but it was painfully obvious that unless they moved fast, they would soon be in range of that gun.

'You'll have to leave me,' gasped the girl through teeth clenched in a spasm of pain as she tried to run on her injured foot. 'You've got to get this information back to my father. He'll know what to do. It's far more important than either of us.'

'Nothing doing,' Carradine said harshly. 'Here, I'll carry you.' Before she could utter a word in protest, he had caught her up, draping her over his shoulder. The breath grasped harshly in his chest. He could feel his heart pumping violently against his ribs as he ran on. In front of him, the green stretch of the valley seemed to roll on to a far horizon which was as distant as it had been when they had first burst out of the cave. His face twisted into a grimace with the extra effort as he stumbled forward. Another burst of fire gave him the strength for an added effort. In front of him, he noticed with a sinking sensation that the ground rose in a grassy slope. There was nothing for it but to keep on running until he dropped and a burst of fire from the machine-gun finished them off. One thing was certain: he would not surrender to these men. He preferred to go out quick and clean, and hoped that if it was the only alternative, the same thing would happen to the girl.

The thought of her in the hands of those things back there appalled him. He staggered to the top of the slope. Through blurred eyes, he stared in front of him. There, less than thirty yards away at the bottom of a stretch of shingle, lay the water's edge and the boat just a few yards to his right. Without pausing to glance around to see how close that tank was, he ran forward, feet crunching in the shingle. The stones and shells cut his feet but he was scarcely aware of the pain.

They reached the boat. Gently he helped the girl into it, clambering in after her. Pray God that the engine would start right away. If it didn't, they didn't have a chance. That thing could only be a couple of hundred yards behind them, hidden from sight by the grassy ridge, but with the clanking thunder of its approach loud in his ears.

He jerked on the starting rope. For a moment nothing happened. Savagely, cursing under his breath, he tried it again, his fingers slipping on the rope as he hauled on it. The engine popped, spluttered, then caught with a resounding roar that echoed back at them from the rocks.

Leaning forward, keeping his head low and motioning to the girl to do the same, he took the boat out into deeper water. The water boiled white behind them as they moved away from the shore. Turning, he had a quick impression of the metal juggernaut climbing into view over the ledge. He could make out the head and shoulders of the man crouched behind the gun; saw him waving his arms and gesticulating wildly. Then he fired another savage burst that whistled evilly over their heads. Less than a minute later they were out of range of the weapon, moving in a wide sweep as they turned and headed in the direction of the mainland.

* * *

For several moments after Carradine had finished his report, Corella had stared at him in surprise. The look of initial disbelief on his face had now given way to one of wonder. He said softly: 'And all of this has been going on under our very noses and no one had even the slightest inkling of it. It scarcely seems possible.'

'Someone did have an inkling,' Carradine said quietly. 'DuCann admitted that the man with the birthmark on his shoulder was one of our agents. I suppose there will be confirmation from London any time now.'

'It came in half an hour ago,' said the other.

Carradine nodded. 'Somehow he stumbled on it. Whether he knew the whole truth or not is conjectural. He found out that they were building something big under the island in that maze of tunnels and caves in the rock. He bribed one of duCann's trusted men to get him information. That's why they were both killed. Something went wrong with the killing, though. Someone blundered badly. Their bodies were never intended to be found.'

'But they were, and if we had only forced the hand of the police chief we might have got onto this a lot sooner.'

'There's no use crying over something that is in the past.'

'You're right, of course. You say that duCann came back to the mainland. He will have come to meet Varandashky. No doubt it was to discuss the method of your own execution. Now we have them on the run. I salvaged some of the old records concerning those two bodies. I shall use them to force the police to take a hand in this. I shall also drop a word in the right place and see to it that the island is sealed. They will probably send the navy in. I doubt if anything will be left by the time they have finished, which somehow I think will not really appeal to them. Moscow will seem a long way off when it comes to facing a bombardment from a few sixteen-inch naval guns.'

'But what of duCann and Varandashky?'

'Ah yes, they must not be allowed to slip through our fingers.' The other nodded his head decisively. 'If they are not on the island, they will not be likely to return there when they learn that you have escaped. They will have their own escape route ready. Even though they believe themselves to be secure, they will have prepared plans for such an eventuality as this. I think I know where they can be found.'

'I suggest that we should get there

before they can leave.' As he spoke Carradine got to his feet, crushing out the butt of his cigarette.

'This is really a matter for me,' said Corella. 'Of course I have men I can trust and it will be purely routine work. We have quite an efficient organisation here and — '

'I'd rather be there if you don't mind,' said Carradine.

The other hesitated, then nodded. 'Of course. If you are sure that you are in a fit condition to come? There may be shooting, as you know.'

'I'm quite ready.' There was still a certain stiffness in Carradine's body, but the desire to finish things with duCann and Varandashky was stronger than this.

Ten minutes later, a car was waiting for them in front of the beach house. The sun was setting out beyond the purple hump of the island. Carradine climbed stiffly into the car, leaning back in his seat gratefully. Corella crushed in beside him. He was beaming broadly. Clearly the thought of some action pleased him now that he was being given the chance of showing Carradine what his own organisation could do when the necessity arose.

'DuCann has a house on top of the hill, overlooking the harbour,' he explained as the driver let in the clutch and they moved slowly and smoothly away from the kerb. 'By now, he will have learned of what has happened while he has been here. He will know that everything is lost. If he chose to go back to the island, he will be trapped with the others. If he stays here much longer the police will come and take him away for questioning; and although he will doubtless protest his innocence, he must know that there is too much evidence against him, and the old case of the two bodies in the sea will be brought out into the open again and this time in a more sinister light.'

'So he will try to make a run for it.'

'Exactly. The same applies to Varandashky. He cannot afford to stay any longer. The odds against him are shortening every hour.' He smiled a little as a sudden thought struck him. 'You know, it would not come as a surprise to me if someone else isn't after these men.'

'You mean the police?'

'No, they will know nothing about them yet. They are grossly inefficient when it comes to making an arrest. The news of this failure will soon reach Moscow. You said that they had already made contact with them concerning your capture. They have their agents everywhere. I think that by now, the order will have gone out to eliminate both duCann and Varandashky. Mistakes are not tolerated in the Soviet Union, or among the agents who work for them.' The other's eyes were bright and cruel in the shadow of his face. 'Perhaps if they did, it would save us time and trouble.'

'I personally have a little score to settle with both of them,' Carradine said harshly.

There was a moment of silence in the car. Carradine's voice had not invited further questions and Corella leaned back in his seat and stared straight ahead of him, watching the back of the driver's head. A little later they began to climb along a narrow street, the surface made of large, smooth stones.

They were now in a strangely deserted

part of Overo on the outskirts of the town. Far below them, whenever they flashed past an opening in the houses on the right, Carradine could see the lights along the beach stretched out like a string of pearls in the deep purple dusk. A three-quarter moon had lifted from the eastern horizon, now shining more strongly as the last blazing vestiges of daylight faded from the western sky. The sea was dark. A vast shadow lay on the edge of the land, divided from it by the thin white line of the surf. Humped on the skyline, the island was just visible, like the back of a whale lying out there in the bay.

Corella leaned forward in his seat. 'Slowly now,' he ordered the driver. 'They will undoubtedly be nervous and watchful. We shall have to stop somewhere out of sight and go the rest of the way on foot.'

'What do you intend to do if the police should arrive on the scene the middle of the proceedings?' Carradine asked softly. 'Won't they feel that this is their territory, their responsibility?'

Corella snorted derisively. 'The police?

That is very unlikely. They do not often come here. Also, if my plan is successful, as I fully believe it will be, there will be no question of the police knowing anything. There will be no killing either. I think London would prefer to have them handed over alive.'

'How do you intend to manage that?'

'This!' Corella took a gun from his pocket and held it out in the palm of his hand so that the street lights flashed on it intermittently. 'An extremely useful and versatile weapon indeed. Your armaments branch thought it up for me a couple of years ago, but this is to be the first real opportunity I shall have of testing it fully. You will notice that it has two barrels. One fires the small darts, typical of one of the newer nerve poisons which were originally developed by the Germans towards the end of the war. The larger barrel fires a gas-powered pellet which can knock out a room full of people within three seconds. Once we have our victims, they will be spirited out of the country back to England in a specially chartered plane which is standing by. There will be no questions asked, either here or from the authorities in England.'

Carradine nodded, feeling a sudden sense of admiration for the other. It was obvious that the Chief's confidence in this man was not misplaced.

Corella said sharply: 'Stop here!'

The car braked smoothly and easily to a halt. Corella had his hand on the door handle. He turned his head. 'Do you wish to remain here with the car? There could be trouble, even though I feel we have everything under control.'

Carradine shook his head fiercely. 'I'm coming with you. I've got a score to settle with these men. Besides,' he added, 'this is my assignment — to get Varandashky.'

'My apologies,' murmured the other. He got out of the car. Stiffly, Carradine followed. The street was quiet and there were few lights here. Long stretches of open ground separated the buildings. A cat jumped from one deep pool of shadow to another, eyes flashing a brief jade-green in the darkness.

'There is the house,' Corella said, pointing. 'He is a careful man. It may be guarded.' He waved the men forward.

Carradine stood with the other while the five men entered the grounds from different points and began a swift, thorough search of the garden. Any doubts he may have had as to the efficiency of the small station in Portugal were soon dispelled.

Less than five minutes later the men were back, returning from the shadows by the side of the road. Corella spoke to them rapidly in Portuguese. Then he came back to Carradine. 'They say that the two men are in the house. They are packing cases. It looks as though they are getting ready to move out.'

'Then what are we waiting for?' Carradine moved forward, tugging the gun from the holster beneath his left arm. Corella caught his wrists, shaking his head reprovingly.

'Not that way, my friend,' he said softly. 'Remember, we want them alive if possible. Now follow me and keep quiet.'

They made their way silently through the tall shrubs and palms that grew in the garden border in the mansion. The five men had melted into the trees and except for a vague, fleeting glimpse of something that was slightly more substantial than a mere shadow, Carradine did not know they were there.

'The window,' murmured Corella. He hefted the double-barrelled pistol into his right hand, pointing with his left. There was a single light showing at the front of the house, from the windows next to the wide-pillared entrance. Even from the cover of the bushes he could see the shadows that flitted occasionally across the curtains over the windows; and once, when one of the men stepped directly in front and twitched the curtains aside, peering out into the grounds as if he had heard something and was looking to check, it seemed to Carradine as though the other was looking straight at him; was seeing through the tangle of leaves and branches with x-ray vision and staring him straight in the eye. Then the curtains fell back into place again, but not quite meeting in the middle.

'Let's go,' said Corella sharply. 'We want to get the two of them together. There may be guards around the house who will come running. If that happens, we shall just have to take care of them. Have you got a silencer for that gun?'

'Of course.' Carradine pulled it from his pocket and screwed it onto the end of the long barrel. It made the Luger a little clumsy to handle, but deadened the sound of the gunshot.

Swiftly, they ran across the wide lawn. Seconds later they were trapped against the side of the house, less than three feet from the half-open French windows. Pressing himself against a wall, Carradine drew in several slow breaths, rubbing his left hand roughly up and down the side of his trousers to wipe away the sticky sweat. He gave a final flex to the fingers curled around the butt of the Luger and nodded to the other to indicate that he was ready. There was still no sign of the other five men. They had slipped around both sides of the house in the pale moonlight.

Cautiously, he raised his head and glanced in through the windows, peering in through the narrow gap between the curtains. There was a long table running down the centre of the room and three suitcases on it, their lids open. As he watched, duCann came into view. He was carrying a handful of documents which he thrust carefully into one of the cases. So they were taking their secrets with them. He grinned viciously. This was even better than he had expected. But was Varandashky there with him? Even as the thought crossed his mind, the tall, bulky figure drifted into view behind duCann. Even though he had not seen the other's face clearly before, Carradine recognised him instantly as the man who had tossed that grenade at him from the car outside Burmarsh. So they had the chance of getting the two birds with the one gas pellet.

Corella got slowly to his feet, paused for a moment, and then kicked the French windows open, stepping through into the room. Two pairs of eyes lifted swiftly, staring at them. Two mouths hung slackly open, teeth gleaming faintly in the light.

'Please stay where you are, gentlemen,' Corella said softly. He waved the gun in his hand to cover both of them. 'I trust you were not intending to leave Portugal?'

‘May I ask the meaning of this intrusion?’ blustered duCann. There was a look of pure hatred in his eyes as he fixed his gaze on Carradine; a look of anger blended with one of intense surprise. He waved a hand towards one of the cases. It seemed a purely reflexive movement; but at the same time, when he thought that their attention might be directed at the other’s moving hand, Varandashky went for his gun, his hands snaking beneath his jacket. The gun in Corella’s hand uttered a sharp bark. For a moment Varandashky continued to target his gun, then his body twisted and kept on twisting as he dived down to the floor, shoulder crashing against the table.

DuCann’s reaction was automatic. There seemed to be no reason at all behind it. He took one quick step to the right as Varandashky fell, lunged and then flung himself forward at Corella, arms reaching out to grab the wrist of the hand holding the gun. There was a heavy thud as his body crashed into the other, throwing Corella backward, off balance. As the two bodies went down with

Corella underneath, unable to use a gun, duCann got his fingers around the other's throat and began to squeeze, nails going into the flesh as he thrust downward with all of his strength.

Carradine acted almost as swiftly. For a moment his finger tightened on the trigger of the Luger, the barrel of the gun swinging down towards the back of duCann's head. Then he hesitated. That was no good. They needed this man alive. Swiftly he reversed the gun, holding it by the long barrel of the silencer. There was a sickening thud as the butt connected with the back of duCann's ear. He flopped forward onto his side. Bending, Carradine prised the fingers loose from around Corella's throat and helped the other to his feet.

'That was a move I had not counted on, my friend,' said Corella harshly, rubbing his bruised throat. He stood for a moment looking about him, then walked over to the table. 'I'll have all of these papers taken away,' he said quietly.

The door opened and two of the anonymous-faced men came in. They shook their heads in answer to Corella's mute enquiry.

'No one else in the house,' Corella said, turning to Carradine. 'It begins to look as though they were planning to leave the others behind. No sign of the girl either.'

'Probably back in England. She possibly knows nothing of this, or that her whole world has crashed down around her.'

'What do you mean by that?'

'Isn't it obvious? Her face is well known now. She can go nowhere without being recognised. Sure, plastic surgery would alter that, but she is a very beautiful, vain woman. She would never agree to that, I'm sure of it. Besides, the Reds may decide that she failed in her work. If that is so . . . ' He did not have to finish the sentence. Corella nodded his head slowly in understanding.

* * *

The moon laid a long, silver finger over the ocean. Already one could feel the faint chill of August nights in the air where it had lain hidden during the heat of the day. There was no one on the long stretch of moonlit beach but the two dark shadows standing near the spot where they had launched out into the water earlier that day to sail out towards the island which now lay dreaming on the sea.

'What do you think they will do with all that equipment on the island, Steve?'

'Probably blow it all up, maybe even turn it over to the NATO authorities. I've no doubt their scientists will drool over it all. Anyway, they'll have duCann and Varandashky in London sometime tomorrow morning. We won't be hearing from either of them again, you can rest assured on that point.'

'And you? When do you have to go back? Tomorrow? The day after?'

He shrugged. 'I'll have to send my report off tomorrow morning.' He glanced at his watch. It was after midnight. 'I mean this morning. I'll have a word with my chief. He may feel he can let me have a couple of extra days' leave before reporting back.'

'And you're not in the least bit sorry about what will happen to Solitaire duCann?'

'I think she knew what she was doing when she got into this business. We all know the kind of risks we run; that things can sometimes go against us when we least expect it.'

'You haven't answered my question,' Veronique said softly, placing one finger on his lips.

'All right.' He kissed her firmly. 'If you really want to know, I haven't even given her a thought since I've been with you. Does that answer your question?'

'Well enough,' she said. She had drawn back her head and he saw that she was smiling. 'I think you had better be very persuasive when you talk to your Chief. Tell him it's imperative that you have at least a week in Portugal.'

THE END

Other titles in the Linford Mystery Library:

THE DOCTOR'S DAUGHTER

Sally Quilford

Whilst the Great War rages in Europe, sleepy Midchester is pitched into a mystery when a man is found dead in an abandoned house. Twenty-four-year-old Peg Bradbourne is well on the way to becoming a spinster detective, but it is a role she is reluctant to accept. When her stepmother also dies in suspicious circumstances, Peg makes a promise to her younger sister, putting aside her own misgivings in order to find out the truth.